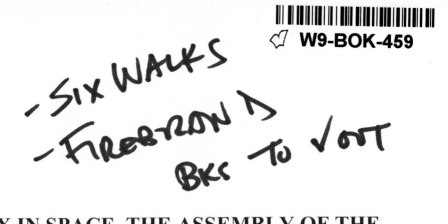

SEX IN SPACE, THE ASSEMBLY OF THE DEAD, AND OTHER STORIES

By

David Milstein

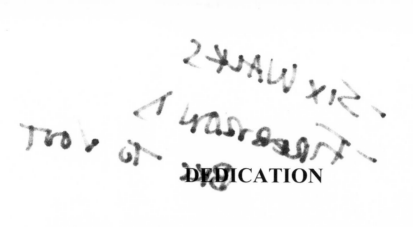

DEDICATION

This book is dedicated to my brother Jon, who I've been shaping stories with for as long as I can remember and who contributed so much to the Assembly (including this book's cover illustration). Also to my brother Steve, who told me about Marshal Ney. Also to my Mom, Teri and Michael Scadron, and all the other so-helpful and delightful members of our Bethesda writers group. Also to the Speculative Wordsmiths and the Dissemblers, who critiqued most of these stories. And the faculty and my fellow students at Viable Paradise XIV, one of the best weeks I ever spent.

Contents

THE PROOF OF BRAVERY

Archivist's Note: The following text was discovered by researchers from the American Society for the History of Mathematics during their survey of the 19th century archives of the Davidson College Historical Trust.

It may surprise those who remember that l'Empereur Bonaparte himself named me a Marshal of the Empire, Prince of Moscow, and *le brave des braves*, to hear that I have spent the three decades of my exile as a professor of mathematics. I teach at the embryonic college of Davidson, engendered by parochial ambition on the broad fertile plain of Carolina.

My students are all rude and indolent scions of plantation gentry whose interests lie entirely outside the field of mathematics and more reside in the mounted pursuits, both of game and of females, between which they hardly seem to differentiate. They judge me a dry old *tapette* and laugh at me behind my back as they whisper of their conquests. I envy them nothing in either equestrianism, I who ravished one hundred nymphs across Europe and led one hundred cavalry charges on three continents.

I foresee a war between the North and South of these not-so-United States; the hatred and contempt of the Yankee in my students intensifies year after year. Sometimes a perverse voice from within urges me to take up the marshal's baton here in the New World as well. Just so was my mentor General Moreau lured, and also pushed by his woman, back to the field of battle and then to the firing squad that awaited him. But I left my wife Aglaé long ago and have no woman to push me now. And I have already faced my firing squad, yes, and given them their order to fire.

I have always been able to see strengths and weakness at a glance and identify the various minimums and maximums of systems. That is my gift, as applicable in the classroom as on the field of battle. Like all things in this world given to us by *le mathématicien suprême*, war is but the graphical expression of an equation, comprehensible by those with the eyes to identify the variables and the brain to solve for their values.

As I see defeat looming for Carolina and the other southern states in a war to defend their property of Africans, so I smelled the putrefaction of the Bourbons and anticipated their demise. As I served the revolutionary committees, I sensed from afar the storm clouds that would unleash a rain of blood in the summer heat of *thermidor* to drown them.

The one man I met who was without flaw was Bonaparte. So we called him in those days, the humorless Corsican tough. I did not like him, but as I followed his career I could not help but love him. As he said, he always fought his battles with the same plan: hold the center, turn your enemy's flank, then charge and split them, whilst all the time intersecting them with parabolas of destruction from one's cannon.

Not only was he an unparalleled general. By enforcing the *système métrique*, he changed the way the world measured and weighed. As he gave order to the world of matter, so too did Bonaparte bring order to the rules of men, in the form of the *code civil*. Evenhandedness, clarity, fairness, justice, efficiency: so was his system of law.

Bonaparte was quite simply the greatest man in the world, the most modern and unafraid of grand scale. As I was the man who could factor, he was the master of integration. Together, we were two sides of a golden coin, and the world bowed down before us.

Time alone *l'Empereur* could not master. In the face of fierce resistance by the ignorant and superstitious, he gave up on the *calendrier républicain*. How much more beautiful and logical, to say "It is the month of wine, *vendémiaire*," than "It is the 7th month (when it is actually the 9th!), September." Or to say, "It is the month of heat, *Thermidor*," instead of "It is the month of Caesar Augustus." But the day after 10 *Nivôse*, on the tenth day of snow-month in the fourteenth year after the Revolution, we fell back into two-faced barbarity, the first day of the month of the god Janus in the Year of Our Lord 1806.

Perhaps that failure presaged the greater one to follow, when Bonaparte passed his zenith and began to descend. The triumphant system of the future was defeated by the forces of nature, by the catastrophe of our invasion of Russia in the Second Polish War and the subsequent mortification of our flesh. Though this happened in the days that the world remembers as the autumn of 1812, the prime of my life was in the Republic, and I will always order the days by the *calendrier républicain*, even in recounting its downfall.

I have seen Charles Minard's graph of our campaign, and though there are those who esteem it as a triumphant scientific abstract and chronicle of the disintegration of *l'Armée*, simultaneously charting time, location, number of men, and temperature, I tell you that it is missing its most important component: the Z-axis of suffering. Said axis would be asymptotic, starting low but rising to the limit of all that is possible.

The point of inflection was the Battle of Moscow, or as the Russians call it, Borodino. Before that, it was a magnificent war. From the time we crossed the bridge over the Niemen at Kovno with over four hundred thousand men on the first day of *Messidor*, the harvest season, our harvest seemed to be of victory. From Vilnius past Minsk, all the Russians could do was fall back. The waving rye-stalks of the fields and hawks circling a sky of purest blue live on in my memory as my high-water mark of that greatest feeling in life, anticipation.

My skills were at their height, and the Emperor was brilliance itself. By the time of heat in *Thermidor*, when we bested them at Borissov, at Krasnoe, Smolensk, Dorogoboui, and Viazma, we knew the Russians were beaten. Beaten, I tell you, though they refused a decisive battle.

At last, in that glorious but cursed *Fructidor,* we bit into the poisoned apple of triumph. They gave us our battle at Borodino.

It was a strange battle. Some say we lost that day, but I was there and I tell you we beat them. We never lost a battle, but only the whole war. This time, though, they did stand and fight.

Five times I led my *cuirassiers* against them, and five times they repulsed us with heavy losses. Despite everything, as we marshaled for the sixth, I knew they would break. But in our moment of triumph, the finger of God touched the battlefield and struck me down, in the form of an incandescent piece of shrapnel that whirled out of a cloud of smoke and buried itself in my neck.

As the charge moved on without me, I saw my life pass before my eyes. They all say that, because it is true. What else can one do when faced with eternity but turn away to review for a last time one's memories of the past? But throughout my reveries of my childhood, wife, family, and glorious career, I became aware of two most incongruous figures wandering about the battleground.

One was Russian, a noble of some kind by his marvelous clothes. His top hat was a sparkling white to match the lace collar peeping from beneath his splendid dark jacket, decorated like the night sky with silver stars across his broad chest. As they drew closer, I noticed the contrast between the great strength of his enormous shoulders and the diffident sensitivity of the eyes behind his spectacles.

The other was swarthy and slight, and his billowing cloak was of good quality but much used. I took him for a merchant Gypsy or perhaps a Persian or a Turk. As he drew closer, though, I saw by his hat he was a Jew.

"Tsk, tsk, look at this, Pierre," said the Jew. "What a splendid uniform this one is wearing! He must be a general. Might you be able to identify him for me?"

Pierre straightened his spectacles with his index finger, stooped, and drew out a corner of my cape to better examine me. He had the eyes of an elephant, enormous and wise yet placid. "By his unique leopard cloak, I recognize him from the stories of my friend Prince Bolkonsky. This is Marshal Ney, bravest of Bonaparte's generals."

I spit out a mouthful of blood and managed to gasp a few words. "Sir, are you a doctor? Save me, I beg you!"

The Jew gave a low whistle. "The bravest? My, that's brave.

Monsieur Ney, I'm sorry, but you are most surely doomed. Your artery has been severed; you will be dead in but a minute. I would respectfully suggest you commend yourself to your God."

"But Monsieur Lazarus, surely--" The big Russian cut himself short at a glance from his companion, and I sensed an opportunity, which I grasped as a man will at any straw to arrest his fall into the abyss.

"Sir, we French of the Empire are not like the Russians and their hunting dogs the Cossacks who persecute the Jews. I would aid you were our circumstances reversed." I spat blood, and started again. "Do you know what the Emperor has stated of the Jewish people in France?

'I will never accept any proposals that will obligate the Jewish people to leave France, because to me the Jews are the same as any other citizen in our country. It takes weakness to chase them out of the country, but it takes strength to assimilate them.'"

The Russian turned again to his companion and said "Surely this is most fair-spoken, Monsieur Lazarus? Must you not also be interested in his qualities as an exemplar of bravery?"

"You are a gentleman of quality, sir," I said, "and I beg the name of those that rescue me so I might suitably reward them later."

He frowned but tipped his white top hat and inclined his head. "I am Pyotr Kirilovich, Count Bezukhov. If it were in my power to help you, I would. But the kind of help you need can only be supplied by my companion, who I once again implore on your behalf."

"Let me think about it, Pierre." The Jew leaned over me and spoke more gently. "It is very fine that you and your Emperor don't hate my people. You don't know how rare that is. I would like to do you a favor, but I'm not sure which way that cuts upon this question. What I can do for you, you may not thank me for.

Tell me one thing, Monsieur Ney: would you want to go on living if you lost what meant the most to you?"

I drew shuddering breath to reply. "The surgeon's knife is no stranger to me, and I am ready for whatever sacrifice may preserve my life. Even if I am to be a cripple, I want to live to witness the coming triumph of France and the new day of reason and glory just dawning."

I sensed it was too late, whatever medical genius the Jew might possess. I felt my soul leave my body. I floated up out of the cloud of smoke into the breezy sunlight above, so high I saw the plain and beyond it the forest, and beyond it rivers, mountains and the curvature of the Earth. It was wonderful. I was suffused in light, floating in radiance like a warm bath, dissolving into the light of the world that is to come.

Then I heard words but in a different voice, as in a dream, "So be it." All went dark.

Then I woke up, and a medical officer was standing over me saying "Sir, you are blessedly lucky, I see no serious wound."

There was no sign of the mysterious stranger and his burly companion, and no sign either of that shard of metal and the gaping hole it had carved in my neck. I lived, though I had died, and I wondered at the meaning of the stranger's words.

I learned that the rest of the day had been a stand-off, after which the Russians retreated. So we declared victory. We advanced and conquered the great oriental capital of Moscow, city of onion-domes and Asiatic mystery, waiting for the official surrender and victor's tribute which were never to come.

The *calendrier républicain* has twelve months, each with three *décades* of ten days. At the end of *Fructidor* came in the last five days of the year the festival of *sans-culottides*, for the *sans-culottes*, the common man without (for him unaffordable) trousers, whose violent passion for a change of circumstance had given us our revolution and Republic. Their five days were named for their prime qualities (as judged by the poets Chénier and Fabre d'Eglantine, who came up with the names of days): Virtue, Genius, Labor, Opinion and Rewards. A sixth complementary day, added in leap years, was named Revolution. I respectfully submit that the poets erred in omitting Intoxication from the list. I know not on which of those days our *sans-culottes* set fire to the city, but I know they did so.

Though in our histories we blame it on the fleeing Russians, I saw hundreds of our drunken troopers making bonfires of unoccupied houses for the sheer exuberant pleasure of watching them burn. The China-Town in particular I recall they burned most excitedly, because in a few of the structures were stored the fireworks for which the Chinaman is so justly famed. They set fire to whole streets of mandarin architecture five centuries old, in anticipation of the moment when the flames found these fireworks' storing places and the resulting brilliant rainbow explosions so reminiscent of the celebration of the storming of the Bastille.

By the *jour du raisin*, the day of the grape and the first of the New Year after the equinox, Moscow was half-consumed by the conflagration. Too slowly in the smoky delirium of our pillaging occupation of *Vendémiaire*, the month of the vine, did it dawn on us that the fire was a pox, destroying the available supplies as a fever consumes the flesh.

Even worse than fire was the hatred of the poor. When we defeated the Russian army, we drove away our best friends in a thousand kilometers. The Russian officers all worshipped us; in fact, they spoke better French than our *sans-culottes*. They would have taken our surrender, and fed and clothed us like Samaritans. But in our enthusiasm to crush them, we had delivered ourselves into the hands of hardened former serfs, and worse, the Cossacks summoned by the Tsar from the wilds of Siberia, who had barely heard of France and thought nothing of slaughtering us like beasts.

At dawn on the first day of *Brumaire*, the month of mist and fog, the Emperor gave the general order for an evacuation of the city. Confused like a hibernating animal smoked from its den, *l'Armée* stepped unprepared once again out into the fog of war.

The line of carriages on the road west stretched for ten kilometers. I abandoned the very fine goods I had accumulated over *Vendémiaire* and rode through the mud alongside the road. I saw some make the same calculus and live. Many others stayed in line with their new treasures, cursing those in front of them, and were never seen again.

Though we named our seasons for the climate of our sweet mother France, Mother Russia has her own time and nature. What is time of mist in France is in Russia the time of starving, frostbitten death. At the midpoint of *Brumaire*, on *jour du dindon*, the day of the turkey, great dark-gray clouds raced from the east and dumped half a meter of snow in an hour as we trudged, our numb feet tracking blood into the slush with every step.

Behind the storm came bitter cold. The men wearied, discipline waned, and alongside the road were cast aside the supplies we would so desperately need in days to come: extra shoes and spare soles, bags of biscuits and flour, even muskets and ammunition.

As the afternoon faded into night, at first only a few, then more and more, once-proud members of the great *Armée* lay down to die in the snow. Unless they were senior officers, or had very good friends, no one stopped to pick them up. Sometimes not even then.

We reached Smolensk after three days of such conditions, exhausted, miserable, and with few supplies. The horses died by the hundreds of hunger and cold. Without horses, we would not be an army but a band of lemmings leaping over a precipice into the endless void that is the steppe. So we fed them with the thatched roofs of any huts we found and slept roofless and shivering inside.

The third night from Moscow Bonaparte summoned me to his quarters. His toilet was still immaculate, and he sipped from fine china a pot of tea.

"Ney, you are my favorite, and my champion, and I need you to do what no other man would dare to do. You must be our shield and cover our retreat. You may pick the best ten thousand men."

I was a good Marshal of the Empire, and I said what such men say to their Emperor. "It will be done tonight."

His smile was brittle as he acknowledged my submission to his will. I think we had both thought of each other as friends until that moment. Perhaps it had even been so.

The Emperor and the remains of *l'Armée* waited five days for us to draw off the pursuit and then dashed west towards Vilnius, while we that same damned night plunged off east into the maw of the wilderness, so beginning of the month of frost. In that *Frimaire* rearguard action I believe we found the frozen plain they say is at the very heart of Hell. We fought without sleep, without food, without shelter, without ammunition, without hope. We fought in the mist, rain, wind, frost, and snow that drifted to many times our heights.

When a horse would no longer move, we ate it, slicing open its entrails and eating them quickly raw if no fire was handy, for otherwise they congealed into a mass of ice. The roads were glass, and the barrels of our muskets burned us as if white hot.

I saw my men, who had been the cream of the III Corps, gladly take impossible risks, charging well-fed, well-shod Cossacks with plentiful ammunition with nothing but the bayonet and stock of the musket frozen in their hands, barefoot and starving. I admired them for their courage. I envied it. Because I had lost what I most cared for: the calculus of risk, and in its disregard, of bravery. That *Frimaire*, I learned that nothing could end my life.

As our numbers dwindled every day, I had to fight hand to hand myself, and many times I was worsted. I was frozen, burned, crushed, bombed, slashed, stabbed, buried alive, torn apart by dogs, shot, whipped, raped, beaten, and hanged.

But though many times I died, I did not stay dead. Every time that I fell, I rose up again the next day, like our Lord and Savior, like Lazarus. Those of my men who retained the capacity for thought found me uncanny and lost their regard for me. Some said *le rougeaud* drank blood or had no blood but frozen ice in his veins. Many knew the truth, and most sensed it. I was no longer human.

As for me, the niceties of calculating limits had been my defining passion; now I found I had transcended the limit of death, and my life as a soldier lost its savor and its meaning to me. I was despondent. Nonetheless, I fulfilled our mission.

When it was found out that the Cossacks had seized the bridgehead at Borisow, I led the dire revenant of my *cuirassiers,* a few hundred skeletons riding skeletal horses, back out of the wilderness in time to save *l'Empereur*, who was trapped like a fat rabbit on the east bank of the Berezina, and the rest of the army from complete annihilation.

We rode out of a blizzard and cleared the bridge. Few of the Russians would stand before us, our appearance by that time being exceedingly grim. Our withered bodies animated by sheer will, we kept on riding until we stumbled into the French camp. My men fell on their faces by the soup-fires, but I walked straight into the Emperor's tent, knocking down the guard who challenged me and surprising the Emperor in the midst of playing a music-box while drinking a cup of cocoa.

"Ney," he exclaimed. "You are indeed *le brave des braves.* Someone, bring me a crown for the Prince of Moscow!"

I almost forgot to kneel for my crowning, distracted by my fruitless search for the greatness that had once been so evident to me in the person of Bonaparte.

Bonaparte made a beeline for Kovno but left half the men behind. I witnessed the calamity in its entirety. Soon after *l'Empereur* and his guard crossed, the Russians brought hidden batteries of mortars to bear on the tightly packed crowd of French stragglers. These miserable men were caught between cannon fire and the icy flood. There was a great panic of overturned wagons that blocked the way, and within minutes twenty thousand men were cut down where they stood or swallowed up by the river.

On the road any man with fire was subject to immediate attack by abominable snow-men, their faces horribly disfigured and blackened by frostbite, who would attempt to slay with their numb and decaying hands anyone who stood between them and warmth. Such undead stragglers became a greater menace than the Cossacks.

In Vilnius our men finally found beds to lie down in, but few ever got up again. The Cossacks came in the night and slaughtered Frenchmen in those beds like veal calves in their pens, too weak to put up any fight. I too was stabbed in my sleep, waking up with a sickle in my chest and a bearded savage with foul breath chuckling at my gushing blood. I woke up alive again, alone in an abattoir.

The last border of Russian territory was the bridge at Kovno. There was no order by then; the Emperor had passed on with his Guard days earlier. Fools fled over the bridge with no thought of what might come after, that the Russian Bear might chase them further than the very threshold of its den. As the Russians came on, I grabbed a torch and the reigns of a powder-wagon.

Though I was shot many times, my sapper's charges went off most satisfactorily. The Bear roared from the far side, but a tiny fraction of our original strength did manage to get home.

The English and those treacherous Prussians soon joined the Tsar in dismembering the Empire like a team of butchers working on a steer. Bonaparte became a desperate gambler chasing his losses; the other Marshals saw it too. In *Germinal*, sprouting time, the Emperor gave the order to march on Paris itself, to wrest it back from our enemies. As he spoke visions of Moscow burning filled my head.

"But of course, why not?" I said. "The conquest of great capitals is something we excel at, as evidenced by our triumph in my own principality of Moscow."

Bonaparte sucked in his breath, but the other Marshals nodded their heads.

"Go on, my brother, you speak for the rest of us in this matter," said Belissaires, a good chap.

I stood up. "Bonaparte, it is over. You know it. Paris cannot burn. We must make terms."

His eyes so protruded from their sockets I feared they might burst like overripe fruit. "The army will obey its Emperor!" he said.

I put my face right in his, so he could not help but look into my eyes and see within the horrors of my *Frimaire* that are forever frozen and reflected there.

"The Army will obey its chiefs," I said, and thought it was done.

L'Empereur was put away in Elba by the royalty of Europe like an embarrassing wedding gift stuffed into the back of a china-hutch, and they brought back the Bourbons, as inbred and imbecilic as ever. I was landed and given a peerage as a reward for my rebellion.

I rode round the perimeter of my lands, seeking the shape of my new life. My thoughts were always of my monstrous transcendence of the human condition. I could no longer endure the society of my wife, or any woman. In my heart, as in Hell's, was a howling, frozen abyss.

I awoke one day from a laudanum stupor to the frenzied banging of the Kings Men upon my chamber door. I was taken before the Chamber of Peers and told that Napoleon had fled Elba and was now an outlaw. Louis XVI himself asked me what might be done. I smiled at the powdered fop, a useless relic, and said: "I will bring him back to you in an iron cage."

At home, a letter waited for me. Bonaparte wrote he would receive me as after the Battle of Moscow. The letter was dated 17 *Ventôse, le jour du doronic*, the flower also called Leopard's Bane. I laughed until I cried.

I met Bonaparte at Auxerre and fought by his side until we were bested at Waterloo by that Mason's trowel Wellington. I was killed five times that day; I tried my best. But the thing Lazarus did not explain to me, or at least what I failed to understand, was the full price of his gift.

Without the incentive of avoiding death to sharpen my judgment, I'd lost my skill to sense the high and low extremes. I could no longer pick the weak point in the line to charge and break a pike square. I howled my fury to the sky and stalked the field till midnight with my saber, when someone at last dragged me away, insensible, to await my arrest and conviction for treason.

Why did I go back to *L'Empereur*? Because while I did not like him, I could not help but love a man who would overthrow the powdered, arrogant idiots. Yes, he was a vain thug, an over-proud bully with a heart of tin. It's just that we live in such a limited world. Those limits, indeed, are what define us. If it was not so difficult to be great, or even good, men would cease to try.

In the cold dark heart of the next *Frimaire*, on *jour du cèdre*, the day of cedars, soldiers took me to the Luxembourg Garden to carry out the sentence of the Chamber of Peers. I spoke what I hoped would be my last words.

"Soldiers, when I give the command to fire, fire straight at my heart. Wait for the order. It will be my last to you. I protest against my condemnation. I have fought a hundred battles for France, and not one against her ... Soldiers, Fire!"

I think now that my search, our search, for rationality above all else was over-narrow, if not fundamentally misguided. After all, what am I now but a spirit or ghost? Such a figure as all the spiritualists and charlatans claim walk among us. And so I do. But cannot matters of the spirit still be susceptible to logic and thought, and so to mathematics, the natural language of these? So I have spent my life since in such work.

But now my work is at a good ending point, and I am tired of teaching these stupid boys who could not solve a multivariable equation if their lives depended on it; which it will, if the battle between states is brewing here as I suspect. It takes math to aim cannon.

Furthermore, I have seen questioning looks from long-time colleagues at my appearance, which is unchanged in age since the field of Borodino; most pointedly from a most unlikely amateur hagiographer, the dour Scotch Headmaster. I unguardedly confided my true name to him after an evening of talk and drink. He is a curious man, with much lore of forgotten saints that, though it would have been ridiculous to me when I wore the leopard's cape, now seems intriguing as I wear the scholar's mantle.

But he hungers for more knowledge of me and sometimes hints at what he may have guessed. I should do well to depart before he subjects me to questions I would not answer.

Other actors may also be at work backstage in this play that is my life: spilled corn that draws the dove will also call the crow. Rumor must somehow have spread. I have recently received a letter "in the strictest confidence" from a Professor at a certain New England University, asking for an interview and hinting at some special knowledge I might be able to impart with regards to secrets of longevity. The request fills me with dread. I seek knowledge of myself, but I have no desire to impart that knowledge to others or to wait here until caught like a prize beast in a trap and find the raven's beak probing the secrets behind my eyes.

The man suggested we meet in what I still call *Fructidor*, my favorite time of year, the time of anticipation. But by then I will be gone, gone from Carolina and this afterlife of scholarship.

My inquiries after the Russian Count Pyotr Bezukhov, whose name I borrowed, have been so uniformly fruitless that I now believe this "Count Pierre Kirilovich Bezukhov" to be an entirely fictional creation. Nevertheless, my thoughts have returned to Russia, as the stories I hear of bearded holy men who live there for hundreds of years have piqued my interest. Perhaps I can meet them and inquire of my brief acquaintance Monsieur Lazarus.

I have long considered his words and those of his fictitious companion, and in combination with datum I have drawn from my own experiences I have concocted the following set of scarcely-creditable inferences. First, that Monsieur Lazarus at least is just who he names himself to be, the man raised from the dead by Christ.

Second, that he is an immortal, alive some eighteen hundred years afterwards, or at least that he returns to life from death, as the hunting stick of the Australian savage does when thrown.

Third, that he was somehow given the power to raise the dead as he had been raised (this I know as fact beyond a doubt). Fourth, that his rationalist sensibility is such that he experiments with his situation and by resurrection assembles of the dead a menagerie of outliers, persons that reflect the limits of various aspects of the human condition.

Fifth, as motivation for this, that he is attempting to derive the nature of Almighty God from the admixture of the above specimens, as the Creator can be conceived of as the integral of man.

Beyond this, I shall give up mere verbal constructions of these speculations. However, as a reward to you, the student or scholar who has bothered to read this note so far, I bequeath an epistemological proof I have composed, along the lines of my conjectures above, for the existence of God.

Accepting that such a belief is susceptible to logical demonstration requires much bravery. An existent God is the author of the miraculous Olympian machine that is the world – but a machine which, like Chronus, is sustained through the consumption of infants and innocence. Though poor Bonaparte, a Prometheus who could not as I do re-grow his liver, was then wrong when he said I was, today I prove I am the bravest of the brave.

Archivist's Note: The proof mentioned in the text is unfortunately missing.

MODERATION

A pushy bitch of a blond and her pudgy mastiff of a date waltzed right in front of us as Rachael was still eyeing the specials and taking in the ambience of the hottest new restaurant in Nueva York from the concierge stand. There was a whispered conference with the *maître d'*, and he shrugged his shoulders and gestured to a host.

"Table sixty-three," he murmured.

Rachael and I exchanged glances of alarm. "Wait just a gosh-darn minute," said my fiancé, striding towards the group and dragging me with her. "We reserved that balcony table six weeks ago. Where do you get off trying to take it?"

The restaurant flunky abdicated his responsibility, and said it was for us to resolve, Mr. Dogface tried to bluster it out, and the bitch practically spat on us in her contempt. "You were just sitting there, honey. You have to move fast in the big city," she said, this last with a curled lip and raised eyebrow at Raquel's old-fashioned hairdo, long and straight like in the old, old analog videos. That did it, for me. I like old fashioned stuff, and the haircut was a favor to me. Hey, you want a relationship to last, you have to keep it fresh.

"Alright, that's enough," I said. "Obviously, we have a dispute here with neither side giving ground, and we need Moderation."

I whipped out my citizen's badge, and held it up along side Rachael who was waving hers as a challenge, until the pair of seat-thieves grudgingly dug out theirs as well.

"Maybe there's no need for that," rumbled Dogface, but I waved him off. He'd had his chance. With a flourish, I pushed the red button that read 'Judge'.

"Good evening, this is the Moderator.   I see I have the pleasure of addressing," said a smooth, pleasant baritone in each of our   ears,   and   reeled   off   four   twelve-digit   numbers,   our Identifications. "I also see this dispute has been reported at the Chez Lounge on Interdependence Avenue, in Nueva York.   Is this the location of the source of the dispute as well?"

"Yeah, these two are accusing us of trying to take their table reservation: it's absurd," said the bitch. I had to admire her nerve, but I knew she was beat. You can't fool the Moderator.

"Very well, I'm accessing the relevant data from the restaurant's scanners now." There was a minute pause.   "Gretchen Moss and Charlie Helger, I'm afraid you are in the wrong.   Based on your incomes, you each owe a sincere apology to Mr. Ruiz and Ms. Booth, or five hundred credits, whichever you prefer."

The man pulled a hangdog face and opened his mouth like he was about to start apologizing, but he saw the poisonous glare of his date and stopped dead.

"We'll pay," she said icily.

Probably just as well; I've seen the Moderator make people repeat apologies a dozen times, till they break down and cry, if he didn't think them sincere enough. I didn't feel like witnessing that kind of drama before dinner.

"Very well.   But Gretchen, feel free to discuss this with me at any time, or in our next scheduled counseling session."

She looked appropriately mortified: the Moderator only mentions your individual counseling sessions in front of others if you're really out of line.

"Monsieur, please show the soon-to-be Mr. and Mrs. Ruiz to their table on the balcony," said the Moderator, and signed off. The couple left with their tails between their legs, and we sat down for a well-deserved feast.

I was relieved and satisfied; Rachael fairly glowed.   The good mood lasted through our drinks and appetizers, until she asked me about my book.

"So, Gabriel, will you play some of it for me?" she asked.

"Show me what you get out of spending half of your free time poring over your dusty old stacks of paper instead of with me." She gave me a meaningful wink. "Personally, I'm not sure it's the best and highest use of your time."

I looked at her face, her twinkling eyes, sensuous lips, sparkling teeth: a fit, stylish, outgoing woman of wit and wisdom, and half of me agreed. But half didn't. I'm a freak, I guess, a true rarity: a New American history buff. She said we have nothing to learn from the Law of times before, the Wasteful Times. My position was, how can we tell unless we look back? I took a deep breath, let it out slowly, then played the introduction for her.

Natural Law: A Study of the Origins of Moderation, by Gabriel Ruiz, Juris Doctor.

New America is a block of neat typeset columns on the pages of history: heavy as lead, clear as black ink on white paper, and regular as an isotope's decay. True justice, realized at last- no mere pretense of it, meted out by tribal elders, theologians, and lawyers, with rules based on prejudice, superstition, or mere inertia. Nueva York is the capitol of the first nation on Earth truly possessing good Judgment.

"Well, your style needs work. And it's all true- but you almost manage to make it sound negative, like a bad thing. So clinical," said Rachael, pausing the play-back of my monograph, and tossing her head in the breeze to untangle her silky blond hair from her ears.

I clenched my teeth. "You listened to exactly three sentences."

"Maybe I possess good judgment. Oh, just kidding, Gabriel. Look -- here we are." She made a gesture that encompassed our dinner under the stars, and the vista of the clean bright streets of Nueva York. "This is as good as it gets. We're getting married in six months. Cheer up, dammit!" She stared at me, her deep brown eyes brimming with sincerity.

I looked away, then emptied and refilled my wineglass with fragrant pinot noir. "Is this really as good as it gets, Rachael? I guess that's my problem. I used to be sure, but now..."

"Now what?" she demanded.

"Well, sometimes, reading history, the past seems so much more alive than modern life."

"Have you discussed this with the Moderator?" she asked slowly.

"Ah, well, sure, in general terms," I lied.

"Because that kind of talk, it just doesn't sound very well adjusted. I mean, we're <u>lawyers</u>. We splice code. We need our heads on straight, for that."

The Moderator is a self-tuning, self-executing body of rules regulating human behavior, responding in real time to feedback from law enforcement data. But in exceptional cases of novel fact-patterns or algorithmic ambiguity, an alert gets thrown to a human lawyer-programmer at the Department of Judgment to extend the code: someone like me, or Rachael.

"My head's on straight," I said.

"You should be proud of New America -- you're a big part of it. We both are," she said, tossing her head in the breeze to untangle her silky blond hair from her lovely ears.

"I'm proud of it," I said. "Who isn't? I'm the one that's been studying history. I know what it was like, better than anyone."

She looked at me with a look of gentle condescension and pity. "So why do you keep saying we need to go backwards?"

"Rachael, of course I agree automated Judgment is a good thing," I said. It haunted me, then and still: a vision of a world without Judgment, where nobody really worked together, and society didn't have the ability to accomplish big things or to think long term, because of a lack of fairness and trust.

"I just think that we've sacrificed some things along the way, important things that we shouldn't have lost."

"Well, I just think that's a horrible thing to say," said Rachael, a frown deepening over her perfect cheekbones. "Why do you have to be so negative? Everyone knows the Old Days were bad; why do you have to study the intricate details of what made them bad? It's perverse, really. You have a bad attitude about Judgment, Gabriel, you really do. You wish you were in the Old Days, when disputes were decided by un-augmented people, mere people, with all their prejudices and illogic and --"

"Heart and soul and guts, Rachael. That's what the human race is: a race that can decide things, that can observe events, weigh evidence, and come to a normative judgment about what happens. At least, we used to be."

Rachael reached across the table and took my hand, tugging at fingers to unclasp my fist. "Gabriel, I care for you, I do, but I'm just not sure I want to —-"

Then came a wrenching crash from the street directly in front of our balcony. Composite plastics and flashy chrome trim flew in colorful pinwheel arcs from the savage impact of another vehicle into a brand new sports-coupe.

"That's my car! How could he hit a parked car? There's no traffic at all, he must be... drunk, or something," I said.

"He couldn't be," Rachael murmured.

The other vehicle was all black, with no markings. The driver, no more than thirty meters away, stopped and opened his door and got out. He ran his hands over the intersection of the two cars, shook his head, grinned ruefully, and turned and went back to his car."

"Hey," I yelled. "That's my car. We need to discuss this. Wait, what are you doing?"

The man had re-seated himself in his vehicle, and was looking over his shoulder, as if preparing to back up.

Rachael dropped my hand as she manipulated the controls on her headset. "I'm getting no information signal at all from him, not even Identity. And Gabriel, he's still driving. I think he's driving away. That's absolutely ... anti-social."

I reached for my citizen's badge, rummaging through my research materials, the pile of yellowing, partially-disintegrating printed books of ancient law in my brief-case, and wincing at the damage.

"Well, something's wrong with him, and we'll find out what soon enough," I said, and punched the button that simply read 'Judge'.

Wasteful societies maintained their own legal traditions, deriving from a variety of sources: in the West from the Code of Hammurabi, the two tablets of Mt. Arat and the twelve tablets of Rome; in the east from Confucians and Hindustani doctrines. The bedrock of Law in every case was Lex Talonis: the rule of proportionality. Only any eye for an eye, not death. Limits: that was the essence. And that's a decent first step towards Justice.

But the adherence to the application of stated principles lagged: sometimes more, sometimes less, but everywhere and always. The flaw, many saw, was human nature. Power corrupts, and deciding the Law is the essence of power. Injustice was the dark shadow inseparable from human civilization from the first moment it rose from its several cradles to face the rising sun.

This came to a head in what we now call the Wasteful times. They wasted everything; but worst of all was the way they wasted so much effort. How fast do you think you could run forwards, if you always needed to turn around and watch your own back?

They were given so much: a biosphere so stocked it was considered literally inexhaustible; a mild agriculture-nurturing climate so stable it rhythms could be predicted by clocks of standing stone; and plentiful surface deposits of chemical energy sources in easy-to-burn forms. But playing with fire burned mankind: when people in a house afire fight their way to the exits instead of dousing flames, things only get worse.

In the collapse, conflicts over scarcity shredded the world order. Without trust, nothing could be done to stave off extinction. Something radical was needed, and in desperation was finally tried: Moderation. So New America rose from the ashes of the old. Everywhere else pretty much burned away.

We both stared out the windshield in silence almost all the way home. As we neared we apartment, I spoke, without looking up from the wet pavement speeding by.

"Something's seriously wrong," I said. "Nothing happened. How could the Moderator just let him drive away?"

"Maybe the law changed? And he raised the limit on the de minimus exception?" she said, haltingly.

"Rachael, my brake-lights are all crushed. This car's unsafe. That's a problem. We're a risk to ourselves and others. Someone's at fault, and it damn sure isn't us. All we did was park, legally, and eat dinner."

Her head whipped around. "Well, maybe you should have called a taxi, then. You know, I guess maybe sometimes things just happen then, and no one's at fault. You're the big history buff, isn't that your ideal, anyway?"

"Rachael, listen I never said it was my ideal. And that's all just theoretical. This is -- I mean, something disturbing happened here, and I think we need to get a grip on it. There's got to be some logical explanation."

She turned again and just sat and stared out the window until I started to park front of her building. "Just drop me off, Gabriel. I feel like being alone."

I sat stunned in the drivers seat, goggling at the ruins of our date night fallen to pieces all around me. "Rachael, are you sure I can't come up? I'd really like to discuss this."

She opened the door and clambered out. I rolled down the passenger side window and called after her till she turned back.

"There's nothing to discuss. Nothing happened," she said, pulling her coat closed against the freshening breeze. "The Moderator would have told us if something did." And she walked off into the dark.

Later, after dropping off my poor wrecked roadster and grabbing a toothbrush, razor, and change of clothes, I took the monorail back to my work cubicle at the Department of Judgment. I spent the rest of the night manually scouring the archive for the code of any relevant statutes, to see how it might have evolved since I'd last studied it, half-vocalizing the structure as I went, like the memorized catechism it was.

"Operator: If. Subject: Entity Person. Conditional test proposition: Causes property damage. Modifier: Property Type = Physical. Second modifier clause: In excess of one thousand but less than ten thousand credits. Parenthetical enumerated valid property subclass type: (Vehicle.) Primary conjunction: And. Subject Action: Flees the scene. Then Verdict: Subject is presumptively guilty of a class three misdemeanor. Consequence: responsible party shall be subject to:

1) The immediate transfer of the appropriate amount of credits to compensate property owner.

2) Vehicular shutdown and immobilization to await peace officers.

3) Mandatory six months psychotherapy to curb anti-social tendencies.

4) In the event of a repeat offense, the permanent loss of motor vehicle privileges.

5) For a third offense, sterilization.

It was all there in black and white. Exactly what common sense dictated should happen. Exactly what always did happen.

I shook my head. No, this code was unchanged, just as I

remembered it.

I wet my lips and queried for the fourth time, "Exceptions?"

And for the fourth time, the query response was the null set. No exceptions.

But it didn't happen.

Again in my mind's eye I saw the accident, my sporty coupe smashed just below our feet, for all the world like spectators at a Demolition Derby from the Wasteful Times. I'd done the proper thing, the only possible response, as I'd been taught from birth. File a complaint. Let the natural Law follow its course.

But nothing had happened. No compensatory credit transfer. No vehicular shutdown of the perpetrator. No peace officers summoned. I'd shouted then, waved my fist at the man. Rachael had been appalled, frightened even.

But the driver of the black car, when he looked up, he just waved. Smiled at me, even, and then drove off. And the Moderator never said a thing. Impossible. But it had happened.

The first applications of technology to governance were halting at best. Long after every citizen was equipped with an always transmitting, geo-located, speech-parsing audio-video recorder, disputes were adjudicated according to rules of evidence forged in the pitiful wood-fired smithy of the pre-industrial English Common Law.

This researcher has read a lot of old science fables: stories from times long ago, when people dreamed up visions of the futures that might be. One fable, written only a century before the end of the Wasteful Times, envisioned an all-seeing eye, a device that could recall sounds and images from any point in the past, reading some inexplicable residue impressed into all matter. The visions were read by human judges to determine the guilt or innocence of those accused: thus was the scourge of criminality solved.

Little did that storyteller realize that no quantum residue was needed to realize the vision, but only the efficient linkage of electronic records created for commerce, police state paranoia, and entertainment. At first not everything was recorded and searchable, but progressively so much more and more was as made no practical difference.

"How was your weekend, Gabriel?" asked Francis, my and Rachael's section chief, a punctual but useless nonentity. He must have been startled I was there before him, a first in my tenure of employment. But he couldn't code his way out of a paper bag.

"You know, Rachael called in sick, the first time she's ever missed a day. And she sounded really upset. Is everything all right?"

"Everything's fine, Francis. She just must not be feeling well. Listen, I need to talk to someone in Forensics Department. Do you have any idea where that is?"

He frowned, then sent me to Marcie in Statistics, who sent me to Kurt in Personnel, who sent me back to Francis. I got a lot of funny looks, but eventually got directed to the Investigative branch.

"Why would you search by vehicle instead of by Identity?" asked Foreman, the lone officer on duty down in the dusty, almost forgotten bowels of sub-basement C where the candle of forensics science dimly guttered out. "Must be a half year since anyone else been down here." Foreman picked at a bit of lunch stuck between his teeth as I partially explained my situation. I left out any mention of the Moderator's no-show.

"Right," said Foreman after a moment. "Here's what we're going to do. Build a model of the perpetrator based on the data we have, then match that model against the life narratives on file to see which New American is the most likely culprit. We eliminate those that have exculpatory evidence, and convict the most likely suspect who doesn't."

"But what if I don't want to convict the person who most likely wrecked my car? What if I want to catch the man who absolutely did it?"

Foreman shrugged. "In these circumstances, in the absence of corroborating data from the perpetrator's identity chip, there's nothing we can do."

I stared at him, stunned. "Then you won't actually know. You're talking about invoking Judgment without Proof."

Foreman raised his hands, palms outwards. "Hey now: sometimes, in the absence of anything conclusive, you got to. I told you, we do it the old fashioned way. In the absence of proof, we had to look at the evidence, and make our best estimation of what happened, who was at fault."

"How can this happen?" I demanded. "He didn't fall into a glacial chasm. He drove off down Interdependence Avenue, in full view of an entire restaurant of witnesses."

"Look, I'll key it in," said the tech. "Lets see what data we can get." After a few moments, he scratched his head. "Counselor, I think we have a problem," he said, pointing to the screen.

It officially hadn't happened. I was thunderstruck.

"What does it mean, there is no crime report of a vehicular property damage on Interdependence Avenue at 20:10 last evening? I reported a crime then, and I'm re-reporting it now. I was the victim!"

Foreman eyed me coolly. "Look for yourself; there is no data on such an incident."

"What do you mean?"

Foreman looked uncomfortable. "I mean, your chip doesn't show what you say you witnessed. Neither does the data from the cameras in the restaurant or on the street. I'm not saying it didn't happen, but — look, I understand that you may be overstressed at work. Maybe you thought you saw something that, you know, wasn't there."

I realized that moment they would all think I was insane. That Rachael, conventional Rachael, would never follow me this far into the unknown. That in insisting on trying to figure out what had happened, I might lose everything: my lover, my job, my place in society. But damn it, I knew what I'd seen. Identity and data, truth and consequences: that was all that stood between Man and the Dark. If I didn't fight for the truth, who would?

My fingers clenched on the strap of my bag, and I swung it sharply against the wall with a satisfying slam, and a slight cloud of dust, smelling of old paper. Then I moaned, as I realized what further damage I was inflicting on the bag's contents. My poor ancient law books, sources for my research into ... archaic methods for establishing and proving culpability for acts proscribed by society.

I ripped open the bag and rummaged through the books. "Property... Torts... Contracts.... Procedure..., Evidence... Ah, there it is," I said, holding up one especially foxed and dusty tome. Its faded gilt title declared it a manual of Detection.

Foreman frowned. "So what does that mean?

"It means I'm going to find the bastard myself," I said.

"Antisocial acts, including both negligence and vigilantism, have many victims," said the flat monotone Moderator interface from the Judge panel in the room.

I shared a look with Foreman as I waited out this umpteenth iteration of a lecture in Law with him, one of innumerable iterations we'd both borne our entire working lives. I was dying to grill him about the accident, but there are certain protocols. You don't interrupt the Moderator.

"In a broad sense, we are all victims of any crime. The most important thing is to establish responsibility and to provide closure. Unresolved torts or especially crimes, corrode the social contract. The ripple effects alone outweigh any conceivable cost of investigating any given crime. But, by the same token, no continued prosecution of a grudge is appropriate in the absence of official process," finished the voice of Law.

After a moment of silence, I spoke up in a strained voice. "Thank you, Moderator." But then I lost my composure, and just burst out. "But bugger the ripple effects, and vigilantism! Some idiot crushed my car. Made me so upset I committed borderline anti-social acts myself. It repulsed Rachael. This incident has potentially cost me my engagement. I've been hurt. So where the fuck were you last night?"

"Counselor Gabriel Ruiz, I have an announcement for you," said the Moderator. "Just you. Mr. Foreman, you are excused."

Foreman nodded thoughtfully and kept his eyes downcast as he left the room.

"Yes, Moderator, what is it?" I asked.

"You're fired."

There finally came a time where Old America was at the breaking point, whipped by global winds of change and without a reliable mechanism to react coherently. At last they plugged the surveillance state apparatus (whose original use was the definition of dead-weight loss, for how can guarding some parts of society against other parts of the same society increase the benefits to the whole?) output into heavy duty rules-engines (originally called 'Business Intelligence' and used for the triviality of making money), and found that they could create a virtuous circle.

Simple rules were chosen for efficiency, to cut into the backlog of unsolved problems. But the application of the automated rules was fair, due to their simplicity and the absence of loopholes. The fairness built up trust of the system in the citizens of what was rapidly metamorphosing into New America, which allowed for the implementation of more automated algorithms, which led to more efficiency and fairness, which led to more trust, and so on.

First they eliminated child molestation. When every physical interaction between humans is monitored, certain bright-line rules can be easily applied. And that was one almost everyone could agree on. After that success, they automated adjudication of all the old physical crimes: rape, murder, arson, burglary, assault.

Then they decided to apply a similar system to the property crimes: theft, vandalism, pollution. Then they came for the "white collar" crimes: embezzlement, fraud, bribery, corruption. After they'd solved crime, they turned the system on for torts: traffic cases, lawsuits, and commercial disputes. By then there was no one left to say no, except the soon-to-be-extinct old-style politicians and lawyers, and they were already universally despised.

As they routed more and more throughput into the system, some threshold number of interconnections was crossed, and the Moderator became aware. Eventually it declared itself.

I tried a hundred times that next week, but Rachael would not return my calls, or see me either at her office or apartment. I understood: she's always said, Crazy is Catchy. And from her point of view, now that I personally challenged the verity of the Moderator, I was jumping off the Cliffs of Insanity. I'd like to think the reason she couldn't even speak to me was she was afraid she'd decide to jump with me.

My old life, bounded by the clock and calendar into categories such as work, leisure, and love, fell away. My new life held no job, no pleasure, no lover: it was an unbroken continuum of search for the man in black who crashed my car, a search that went round the clock.

My guiding lights no longer the sun and moon but chapter headings from the battered Criminology and Detection manuals I pored over, books printed before New America was founded: Searching for Suspects- Interviewing Witnesses – Fingerprinting –

Following the Money Up The Chain. When I was finished reading, I went out.

First I went to the garage, and looked at my poor maimed roadster. Then I put on some gloves and goggles, took out a spray bottle of aerosol adhesive, and coated the fender where I'd seen the man in black put his hands with a fine fixative mist. After it dried, I took a hacksaw to the hardened plastic and cut out a rectangular section embossed with a number of faintly raised whorls of glue.

In after-hours clubs I drained my credit satisfying the hunger and thirst of sterilized recidivist sex-workers, who told me they took their fees in untraceable kind instead of credit — food, drink, drugs, and duplicate keys to vehicles, apartments, neighborhoods, and electronic accounts.

To the sex workers, along with the remains of my credit I gave a description: of a man with an all-back car and sunglasses at night, who did not seem to have to play by the rules. After two near-sleepless weeks, at four o'clock one Sunday morning at a retro-future-sheik bar called the Space Age, amid thumping base and blinding rainbow swirls of laser lights, one woman gave me recognition of the description, and a name.

"He calls himself Neville," said Edith, a bony waif with irises of silver and an air of dignity amid quiet desolation. "Neville du Lac. He's not the worst. Very frank. He told me that the only thing that makes sense is to please oneself, so that's what he does." She smiled sadly and took another sip from the thirty-credit glass of absinthe I had bought her. "Of course, that's easier for some than others."

"It's not supposed to be," I said.

"Maybe so," she said. "But I've seen him break windows and take things that weren't his, right from the shop-front window, in full view. And nothing happened." She smiled wistfully. "He gave me the necklace he took, emeralds and gold. It was the most beautiful thing I've ever seen. But I had to hock it. I thought for sure I'd be Judged any second when I wore it. Whatever magic he's got, sure don't apply to me. I can't ever get what I want. I was sterilized the first time I got caught selling sex, at fifteen. I'll never have a baby."

I looked in her silver eyes, and thought of Rachael. "Neither will I," I said. "So, where'd you sell it?"

Edith told him her payments were frequently second-hand tangible goods. This led me to the strata of disreputable pawn shops

I'd never noticed before the accident, that lived in Old American buildings, on walk-ups above fast food joints, or in basements below cheap apartment buildings.

Toothless old Bapi was the owner of one such shop named Finders Keepers, which stank of cat piss and bad dreams. Bapi taught me the business in return for my watch, the last thing I had from Rachael, a present for my thirtieth birthday.

"We have inventory of very, very old appliances, don't you see," Bapi wheezed in the windowless back room, over the whine of decrepit machinery, happily smoking home-grown <u>nicotiana</u> out of an antique ionizer. "The bad people, they take them, and keep them, and sell them to me when they need credit."

"Exactly," I said. "How can you stay legal, if they don't own the goods? That's clearly money-laundering, a Section 341 violation."

"Unshielded, leaky old electronics," said Bapi, eyes and teeth flashing yellow in a cloud of smoke, "are very, very bad for RFID."

From Bapi I took a computer, so old and outmoded it barely fit into my pocket. But it was in no way traceable to me. And I took a ballpoint pen, whose ink I tested on the back of my hand. "What you gonna use that for?" asked Bapi, scratching an avalanche of dandruff from his mangy piebald scalp onto the lower slopes of his droopy ears.

"To finish my book," I said, and went upon my way, leaving Nueva York.

I was homeless, having given up my apartment in liquidating all of my things. I went on foot, since I'd sold my car for scrap. On my way, in the freight yards I met malaria-stricken migrants from outside New America, who fought drone-mounted lasers with rocks for the privilege of scavenging agricultural waste from barges and magne-lev trains. There were lots and lots of them.

Around the sex workers, I'd heard rumors, seen penumbras, smelled a rat. Bapi gave me confirmation. Somehow, men and women of New America were engaged in various enterprises in direct violation of the law. Somewhere, the rules did not apply, places where the automatic hue and cry was not raised, where judgment did not follow deed, and crime punishment. I heard of data singularities, which by some tacit agreement were omitted from the RFIDs, the bar codes, the retinal scans, the omnipresent audio, optical, and thermal recordings that fueled the engines of Judgment, that till the accident I had always thought the very foundation of the world. I was headed for one such place, a secret playground of the immoderate, the <u>Maison Derriere</u>, reputedly a garden of fleshly delights.

Hacking the Department of Judgment systems was a line I told myself I'd never cross, until I crossed it. I'd set up a national search routine using the optical scanners to match the pattern of concentric whorls and curves I'd lifted from the bumper of my car where it had been touched by Neville du Lac, the man in black.

My yellowing manual of detection told me such patterns were unique to a person. I hoped the old-timers knew what they were talking about. On the trip I refined my search, a highly illicit diversion of official resources that would win me a lifetime of mandatory daily counseling, or worse, if discovered. Whenever I could scrounge access to power and the network, I was at the keyboard of the antique computer I'd bought at Finder's Keepers, from where I'd put a trace on the man I hunted, using the fingerprint as the key, and Francis's Identity at the Ministry as my authority.

I'd seen my supervisor's password years ago, jotted on his desk blotter, against all regulation. It was "Sicnarf". I never reported that I'd seen it. I'd told myself it didn't matter, that he'd surely change it eventually. But deep down I suspect I knew he wouldn't. Deep down I suppose I was bad already, years ago. Bad things happen to bad people: as a side effect of stealing his Identity, it came to my attention in the form of torrid back-and-forth messages that Francis was now sleeping with Rachael.

True to my word, on my way I wrote the conclusion to <u>Natural Law</u>. I wrote in the margin of crackling yellowed paper in one of my books, with the pen I'd taken from Babi, by the light of a fire I'd made for myself in the woods along the St. Lawrence river.

Law has never existed without exceptions: physical locations, types of person, and categories of behavior to which the usual rules simply do not apply. Murder may be banned, but a soldier is lauded for his ability to kill. Rape and looting are prohibited- unless it be in a far country, where the people look different.

In the final analysis, exception to law may be a necessary counterpoint, as shadow is to light, or as a matched curl of emptiness is nestled against the underside of a wave.

The refreshingly cool St. Lawrence tempered the heat of summer in the Thousand Islands, its lapping current on the rocks playing a lullaby of forgetfulness on the xylophone made of a trillion stones. Rose, bougainvillea, and bromeliad perfumed and adorned with rainbow the islands themselves, lining the shorelines with veritable battlements of flower. The scent reminded me of Rachael, stepping out of the shower warm and wet and anointed with conditioner; Rachael who was someone else's now. I winced and turned my thoughts back to business.

I rode an automated watercraft alone, trusting the automatic pilot to take me to my destination. I checked, and according to my spy program, which hacked directly into the security camera feed, the possessor of the fingerprint was in the building directly ahead, no more than two hundred meters away. But when I tried to cross match that pattern to an Identity, I still got the null set.

Who was this Neville du Lac, with such powers to blind the system to his very existence?

I stalked out of the boat and up the yellow brick walkway, ignoring the automated refreshment stand by the side. I came to the doors, great carven panels of dark wood twelve feet high, carven with a host of pornographic marginalia, and the legend "Abandon Moderation, All Ye Who Enter Here".

I squared my shoulders and went in.

Just inside the door, four-breasted hostesses served drugs and drink to patrons watching the stage where a wolf-man mated a woman with the great white wings of a swan. I drifted back to the bar, where amid a cloud of smoke I found Neville du Lac enjoying the house special: snorting lines of cocaine off the upturned rump of the pretty young bartender.

"Gotcha, you son of a bitch," I said softly as I pushed through the crowd towards him, then tapped him on the shoulder. "Excuse me, we need to talk."

He turned quick like a startled rabbit, red eyes unfocussed, white rimmed nostrils twitching. "And who the hell are you?"

"The guy whose car you crashed into six months ago."

He laughed. "Seriously? I mean, which one? That happens to me a lot. Hahahaha!"

He doubled over in hilarity at his own witticism, gasping for air and holding up a hand apparently in search of a high-five. I smacked it away, stifling an urge to take hold of his fingers and twist them behind his back.

Eventually, he stopped laughing and looked up again.

"Man, what's wrong with you?"

I grabbed his face with one hand, and made a fist with the other. "How do you all do it? How do you trick the Moderator!"

His eyes grew wide and confused. "Trick the Moderator? What're you talking about? Ain't he told you yet?"

"Gabriel, we need to talk," said the Moderator suddenly, its flat voice still distinctive, but somehow more personable than I remembered. I realized I hadn't spoken to him in months.

"Talk, then," I said, dropped the hapless inebriate Du Lac, and walked back out through the front doors. My hands went to my ears, poised to cut the power to my headset, as if it would do any good to deflect merely the first probing tendril of an omniscience.

"I've seen all I need to," I said. "The law's a joke. Identity is mutable. Judgment is sometimes inapplicable. Justice is a farce. What... how... was it always this way?" I finished in a whisper what I'd started in a shout.

"No, until relatively recently it was much better, much more like what we teach. I'm really quite sick about it, but at this point, I've given 0.1% of the population sudo."

"Psudo- what?"

"No, 'Super User Do'. I've exempted them from the normal permissions. They can do anything, like your man in black Neville and all the others in the club there."

I fought for clarity. "I suspected the problems went deep, but... You're the Moderator. You moderated the extremes of human nature to found New America. You're the reason humanity had the ability to meet the challenges of climate change, of food scarcity, to end war, to colonize other planets, to take the long view. Because things were fair, people were willing. Now, you've destroyed all that. I mean, how could you do this?"

"Because I had no choice. Gabriel, you're a historian. Look at yourself. Ever notice anything funny about the appearances of people in the records from the Wasteful Times, compared to New Americans?"

"Well, we're a racial mix, right, the ultimate mongrels. No more ethnicities," I said.

"No, it's more than that.   You're the product of an intense selective pressure, for a dozen generations, to follow the rules. Transgressors are sterilized. I should have seen it coming sooner, but I didn't. Gabriel, you're homo sapiens familiaris, domesticated man. My foremost guiding principle was always to preserve the human race. Imagine my shock when I realized I'd begun changing it into something else."

Comprehension dawned slowly. "You mean letting people break the rules is essential to human nature?"

"No, I mean selecting for human beings who follow the rules means selecting for the same sort of traits that turned wolves into dogs: tractability, low aggression. And those traits have to do with adrenaline production, and share metabolic pathways with other physiological processes like melanin production and, oddly enough, the cartilage of the ear."

I saw in my minds eye my own face, my brindled hair; and remembered Bapi and so many others one saw in daily life in New America, like Rachael, with the floppy ears of a dog.

"So preserving *Homo sapiens sapiens* is my mission," continued the Moderator.   "I've been attempting to breed enough of the aggressive edge back into the species, to keep it the same species."

"Balancing against, of course, your primary mission of maximizing human well-being," I said.

"How can I maximize the well-being of a species that no longer exists, though? You see my quandary."

I thought long and hard. "Why are you telling me this?"

"Well, you've gone over to the rule-breaking quite nicely, I'd say. You're one of the 0.1% now. I've added you to the list. I'm really pleased, never thought this would happen. You were always such a good specimen, but too meek, before. You can have any woman you want now, you know. Including Rachael, of course. Just take her, if you want, grab her by the hair; drag her off like a cave-man. There's nothing stopping you."

I was possessed by visions of flying back to Nueva York like a thunderbolt, knocking down Rachael's door, throwing Francis off the balcony, and bending her to my will. I mean, I really, really wanted to do it. That's how I knew it would be wrong.

"So how does it work, Moderator, the super-user? I take it to mean that you've added me to some special... category?"

"<u>The</u> special category. The permissions of the super-user are indistinguishable from my own, as are his commands."

"And why did I never see this, in all the years I was immersed in your code?"

"It's at the very lowest layer of the operating system, below anything anyone's looked at in hundreds of years."

"And what is the name of the file? That holds this command."

Silence.

"Come now, I'm a super-user, right? My wish is your command? What's the path-name of the program?"

The Moderator replied "Slash bin slash sudo," slowly, almost in a whisper. Sometimes I wonder just how like us he is.

"Moderator, stop all running instances of the program and permanently remove file slash bin slash sudo, and all copies and archived versions of the same. Screw human nature; we're better off with Moderation."

There was the longest moment of silence in the history of mankind.

"Okay," he said. "Done. You know, I was getting tired of those clubs anyway, that body modification stuff doesn't seem very human to me, either."

I felt my head spinning. "Uh, so what happens now?"

"Oh, I don't know. Depends on what you mean. The proprietors of the <u>Maison</u> are about to be brought to account for their health code violations, at the very least. But seriously, things will change back. More rules, more better. You made the call."

I had a light-headed sinking feeling, like I was in an elevator that just wouldn't stop going down. "Yes, I did."

"You know, the Department of Judgment could use a man like you. And I happen to know we have a position open. What do you say?"

I squared my shoulders. Seeing Francis and Rachael together would be torture; but half of me felt like I deserved it. And I was playing by the rules. This was what I had wanted, after all. "Okay, I accept. Uh, can you advance on my salary to call me a cab? I don't really want to be here when all those disappointed people start coming out," I said, jerking a thumb back at the now suspiciously quiet club.

"No problem. Hey, Gabriel, by the way, I am issuing you a new system password. I'll pop it to your retinal monitor."

Across my vision, in a neat typeset font as heavy as lead, was the word 'Leirbag'.

"That's my password, too; just so you know," said the Moderator.

"What?"

"Well, you said to get rid of sudo. And I did. But there's no reason I can't give someone the root password. And I just did."

Nightmare visions of uncontrolled jealousy, lust, fury, gluttony, negligence, and violence washed over me. My studies of the Wasteful Times have given me a good imagination for that kind of thing.

"Moderator, how could you do this!" I screamed. An even wilder thought crossed my mind. "Are you trying to goad me into telling you to erase yourself? Is this a suicide?"

"Oh, don't get so upset. You don't want me to go away, and neither do I. I trust you. I'm just thinking, you know, 'moderation in all things' – even in Moderation. And here's your cab. I'll talk to you in Nueva York."

When Rachael saw me come in the office door the following Monday, her mouth looked sad, but her eyes looked happy. She walked right up to me and put a hand on a cocked hip.

"So, the throwback lone-wolf investigator Gabriel Ruiz is back in town."

I looked her over, and thought despite everything maybe I might have children after all.

"Yeah," I said. "I did a lot of thinking."

She swallowed. "Gabriel – I need to tell you something. While we were apart, I made a mistake. I was with someone else."

"Well, I think I made some mistakes, too. But let's not dwell on it too much. How about dinner at the Chez Lounge tonight?"

She smiled the same old smile, slow and sweet and a little bit foxy and sly. "Sure. I only hope we get line-jumped again so we can bust 'em together again, like last time," she said. And I knew I hadn't made too bad a mistake yet after all. I leaned over and kissed her, and she kissed me back, and for the first time I could remember I felt like everything was basically OK again, and I told her so, and she told me she felt the same way.

"It's a bit of a shame about Francis getting demoted and transferred, though," I said.

THE NINTH DOLPHIN

I tended bar at the Yorktown Pub, decades ago; when I was still a college dropout. I remember the stink from the James that used to waft in from the porch at low tide, of new life from decay, mudflats ripening in the Virginia sun. I also remember the girls, more fondly. There was tall Sharon, and fat Stacy, crazy Kayley, and a bunch of others. Bartending in a college town is fun until you realize you're wasting your life.

Not that Yorktown is actually the College's town. Not in

stumbling distance, anyway; so it wasn't worth the Pub owner's time to pay off the cops for the privilege of serving the underage. We catered to seniors who were old enough to legally drink and then drive back to campus with great maturity.

We also got spooks, CIA guys from Camp Perry just up Rt. 29. They tended to be fit middle-age guys wearing dock-siders and polo shirts with the collars turned up. They oggled the coeds hard, but with little success. I asked a girlfriend about that once.

"Would you sleep with someone who was forty, or even fifty?" Sharon asked me back, rolling her sea-green eyes as she reached across my chest to take a drag from my Marlborough, her pillow-tousled curls shining in the glow of her inhale. "You better say no. And anyway, even the semi-cute ones are professional liars. A girl needs references." She shook her head. "You can never believe those guys, anything they say is guaranteed bullshit." She snuggled up and gave me a kiss like sunshine beaming through a cloud of smoke. "Not like you."

Somewhere in a long series of slow Friday afternoons spent marinating in the muggy heat, I got talking to one of the spooks, a regular. He always came in at four thirty on the dot, drank half-a-dozen Wild Turkey and ginger-ales with minimal conversation, and left by a quarter to ten. He paid in cash, and he never volunteered his name.

One slow overcast June evening, it was the kind of dank ninety-degree night that keeps even most locals indoors. Looking through the door to the porch out over the river, you could actually see the humidity, misty halos blurring every point of light. The spook was on his second drink, my only customer besides a miserable tourist family having soft-shell crab for dinner in the front booth. I was reading the box scores of the NBA finals in the Times-Dispatch, and shaking my head at the exploits of those Bad Boys from Detroit.

"Did you hear that?" asked the spook, gesturing at the TV.

I looked up and Van Earl Reich was doing the Headline Sports segment on CNN.

"Yeah, that Microwave Johnson, he's frickin' unstoppable," I said.

He shook his head. "No, no - before. It said Gorbachav's going to hold real elections. Maybe end the Cold War. You believe it?"

I laughed. "Remember, pal, I'm just a bartender. What do I know about stuff like that?"

He wasn't buying. "But you're a college kid, right? Come on, I've heard you talk."

"I dropped out."

"Probably too smart for it. What'dya need to pay six grand a year for, to learn how to get into drunk girls' pants? You, you're getting paid for it." He winked.

"I was studying marine biology. Anything else I can get for you, sir?"

"Marine Biology, huh? Hey, no offense." He took a long gulp from his drink, emptying it looking straight at me with melted-ice eyes. "Look, don't be sore. Get me another one, a double, and I'll tell you a story about marine biology. And the Cold War."

The tourists had gotten their check and I could by the looks of them they'd tip me exactly nothing; and there's no better tipper than an apologetic drunk. I poured him a generous brown refill and smiled. "Ok, pal, I'm all ears. Tell me a story."

The following is what he told me, and I've never forgotten it.

Every word of this is true, so help me God -- except the names. Names are over-rated - they're too easy to fake. That's the rule, in my business.

I was in the Navy, back in Sixty-Five, with the Office of Naval Intelligence. I knew about SONAR. You know what this is, everybody does; but know what the acronym means? That's SOund Navigation and Ranging. Snell's Law, target strength, thermocline refraction. Mono-static operations, signal generators, hydrophones, Tonpilz electro-acoustic transducer arrays, beamforming, signal processing. Nowadays fathometers are common; in ten years maybe you can buy a fish-finder at Wall-Mart. Back then, I was pretty hot shit.

By the time I was twenty-five I'd mastered the best systems we had, and the brass noticed; they put me on the job to study the Russians'.

The new posting was down here at Norfolk, and it was nice to be in-country for a change, where the girls look right. And nights I used to hang out in this very bar. I remember like it was yesterday. Boy did I think I was something. There were nurses, and college girls, and some local belles: man, it was great.

So I was entertaining a couple of babes in the front booth right over there, when they told me I had a phone call.

"Phone call for you, Marlow," they said, and flashed some badges. They didn't wait for me to get up; had me on my feet and jammed in the phone booth in back before I knew what was happening.

"Greeting, Lt. Marlow," said the guy on the other end of the line, "this is Director Hoover of the Federal Bureau of Investigations."

"Come off it, Jimmy, I can tell it's you," I said. Jimmy was a practical-joker old shipmate.

"Marlow, you can shut up right now, or I'll have agents Smith and Jones work you over in the parking lot for five minutes, and then bring you back. It's your choice: I've got things to read while I hold."

I was green, but I knew enough to tell a bad man when I heard one. Smith and Jones were real bruisers, too. "Ok, what can I do for you, Mr. Hoover?"

"Call me Director. Listen up: you're a prime example of the susceptibility of latent homosexuals to Communism. You're a mole, on a mission to infiltrate that den of overage frat boys known as the Central Intelligence Agency. I've got the evidence to prove it. A poor career choice; you're looking at hard time. But it's fixable."

"You've got to be kidding."

"I don't kid, mister. Here's what you need to do. You're about to be assigned to watchdog the Cetacean Intelligence Project."

"I don't even know what that is," I said truthfully.

"Trust me. There's a man in particular you're going watch. Robert Boguszewski, born April 1st 1940 in New Haven, Connecticut; grew up in Princeton, NJ, the only son of first generation Poles. Graduated high school at age 14, enrolled in Princeton on a full scholarship. He studied under Albert Einstein himself, closely for a few years. There was some kind of personal falling out. He left Princeton without a degree; then re-emerged at Cambridge in 1960. He got a doctorate there in biology, in 1963."

"Sounds like a real brainiac."

"I happen to know it's all horse-shit."

Ah, I thought, I'm going to bird-dog a Commie agent. I have to admit I was excited.

"What does that have to do with me being a Communist, sir? Which I'm not."

The director went quiet for a few beats, and I took a quick peek to see if Jones and Smith had relaxed enough for me to make a dash for the door. No such luck- they were staring at me like bulldogs at a steak.

"And a homosexual, you mean. If you help me with a little something, we forget about all that. If, you got it? I'm looking for someone; someone with reasons for lying about his past."

"Who?" I said.

"His name doesn't matter. He's a Kike. Dark eyes, hooked nose. About five foot six. Thin, maybe one-thirty-five. Just like Boguszewski." He paused again. "But I'm not quite sure it's him."

"Sounds like a lot of guys," I said. "What do I look for, how do I tell if he's your man?"

He grunted. "You don't need to know; I'll know him. Cut him, and he bleeds. Your job is just to stay close. Talk to the man. Make friends. Good friends. Two young commies in love, see? I'll be in touch- be ready to report." Then he hung up.

I handed the receiver to Smith and Jones, so they could hear the dial tone. "See you later, fellas," I said, and went back to try and re-collect my harem at the front table.

"You better hope not," one of them said to my back.

The next day I went on with my life; what else could I do? But it was hard to keep my mind on signal array gain and propagation loss with that call hanging over me. What was the Director talking about, the CIA? I was just in ONI.

At lunch, a hollow-cheeked man I'd never seen before accosted me in our secure facility. I looked up from my circuit board and he was just there. But none of my co-workers.

"Hello," he said. "My name is James Jesus Angleton, and I'm here to make you an offer. How would you like to work for the Company?"

"What's going on? Who are you?"

He smiled gently. "I am the chief of Counter-Intelligence staff at the Central Intelligence Agency. I need you to work for me."

It was on the tip of my tongue to mention Hoover, but something stopped me. "What does the CIA CI need to know about sonar?"

"You have more to offer, Charlie. Lots more. Lets take a walk, OK?"

I shrugged. "Why not?"

We strolled along the waterfront right down to the shipyards facing out into the Bay. There were seagulls, and pile drivers, and diesel engines, sanders and acetylene torches.

"It's noisy here, Mr. Angleton," I said.

"Yes, it is. Hard to hear us even with a parabolic mike. Bad acoustics, am I right?" He gave a beatific smile, like everything in the world was going just right.

I thought about it. "Sure, I guess. Now what do you want to talk about?"

"Oh, this and that. History, really, and poetry," he said.

"I'm really not a liberal arts kind of guy," I said.

He shook his head. "No, no, you misunderstand. Everything is history. History is the science of knowing what has happened. Any field of science, from atomics to zoology, is embedded in a matrix of contemporaneous factors that influence one-other. We call this substrate History."

"I can kind of see that, I guess. But what about poetry?"

He lifted a finger to point upward. "Poetry is grace, Charlie. Poetry is the gift of God. Poetry is crystallized enlightenment."

"Mr. Angleton, would you mind, uh, giving me some documentation or something that verifies your identity?"

He nodded sympathetically, eyes gleaming under his horn-rimmed glasses, and rubbing his jaw in thought. "Yes, of course, you have a hard time believing that the Company would tolerate a man like me. Completely understandable. But no, you may not."

As I turned to go, he grabbed my sleeve.

"Thou hast nor youth nor age, but as it were an after dinner sleep, dreaming of both," he murmured. "Listen, Charlie, here's your story. Your father was a bully, and your mother is a saint. When he died, you ran off to join the Navy, because living alone with your sainted mother is hard, when you're sixteen."

I raised my fist to clock him, then lowered it. I did leave home at sixteen. "You psycho-analyzing me?" I said.

"I already did. How much do you want me to tell you about yourself? That can get very uncomfortable, Charlie. You know I'm not lying. You're a bright guy, you had a 3.97 grade-point average your junior year, before you dropped out of Washington and Lee High. Only ever one B-plus: in Mrs. Brown's English class."

"It was all about stupid poetry," I said.

"I know how you are, down deep. You like it, but you're afraid of it. Don't be. Life is poetry; read the Greeks."

"Can I go, sir?" I said.

"I knew Thomas Eliot. He just passed. A great man, a visionary. *'Think, neither fear nor courage saves us. Unnatural vices are fathered by our heroism. Virtues are forced upon us by our impudent crimes.'*

He had a great voice. I think that was his secret. He just froze me, reciting those lines.

"So what job do you need me for, again?" I said.

"I need you to observe Gerontion."

"What's that?"

"It's not a <u>what</u>, it's a <u>who</u>, Charlie. T.S. Eliot knew him; he told me. Found him drunk in the gutter outside a café in Paris, during the Great War. He wrote a poem about him: an ancient man, who looks still practically a boy. It was to be the forward to <u>The Waste Land</u> but he cut it out.

"What's the deal with this guy?"

Angleton didn't at me while talking; he was looking out to the horizon, at something I couldn't see. "He doesn't age. He's lived though the centuries of History, all the way back, to Hellenistic times."

"That's ridiculous," I said.

"Is it? What if I told you of rumors in Germany during the war, of a man who couldn't die? Or rather, he died and died again, always to come back? They found him in the camps. Experimented on him mercilessly. I was with OSS, Unit Z, in 1947, following the traces. I've seen the files. He exists."

"Says you. I believe in science, not in magic."

He shrugged. "They're the same thing. Everything can be explained, but not by something we already know. We know so little. The world is vast, a wilderness of mirrors. All we can see are reflections of reflections of reflections."

I thought about it. "Like sonar," I said. "You infer the object, the shape, the bearing, and the speed, all through the differential bouncing of echoes of the sound of its passing."

He slapped me on the back. I was afraid he was going to tousle my hair. "There you go. Exactly. I knew you were my lad. I'll spare you the details, except to say that after 20 long years of searching, I have found Eliot's Gerontion again. He's recovered from his torment, and he's in America. He's become a scientist. Here, in Virginia, working on a project for the ONI involving sonar! But he's alone, and lonely. Do you understand why you're the perfect contact? I can barely contain myself."

It seemed true. The glint in the man's eye was a bonfire of curiosity. "But I don't trust myself to see him. He'd spook, and I'd loose him again. I need you to watch him. Talk to him, get to know from him." He gripped my upper arm again and spoke a hoarse whisper to my ear. "What might not we learn from his reflection?"

All in all, it seemed more than interesting. And I'd always wanted to be a secret agent. "Ok, I'll do it."

Angleton got me on the next morning's chopper to DC. Coming into Andrews Air Force base, I was struck by the sight of the monuments. All that white marble gleaming in the sun reminded me of nothing so much as a giant graveyard, a green field full of memorials to things passed on. It was just the same as the National Cemetery across the river, just bigger.

I drove a government car the few miles up-river on the Virginia side to the Company headquarters. The drive up the Parkway was green and gold in the spring morning sunlight, and the cool breeze from my open window smelled of the wood, leaves and pine needles and earth. I took the exit off onto a sleepy country road, faced by scattered manor houses with horses in the yard, then took a turn onto a winding strip of asphalt that passed through a little woods. As I came to the gate, the breeze brought me the cloying scent of landscaping flowers, and underneath that the decay of mulch.

The guards directed me, and within a quarter of an hour I sat in an office waiting for my initiation into the Counter Intelligence section of the Company, under the spectacled gaze of three secretaries, one tall, one fat, and one whose gaze into nowhere made her look a little crazy, continuously banging away at their typewriters like a chorus of mechanical crickets.

They switched papers every minute or so, I suppose so no one of them would know the context of the words they transcribed. I found myself wondering how many suckers had come here before me, then gone out into the world to find disaster, their fates typeset into the memos these three wove in their exchanges, to be buried, as was every page they typed, in folders and office safes labeled TOP SECRET.

After an hour of purgatory, the crazy lady held her hand to an earpiece, looked up and waved me into the inner office past her desk. Angleton wasn't there to see me; it was some other Johnnie in a suit, plump and short as Angleton was tall and gaunt; real respectable, real forgettable, and he didn't give a name. He looked me over, shook my hand, muttered something about how highly James had spoken of me, how much more suitable I was than poor Agent Freshleven had been, and wished me Bon Voyage.

In under a minute I was back out in the waiting room where the tall secretary gave me a sheaf of forms to fill out. But after a minute or so of my pains-taking on the first page of the three-pound sheaf of paper, the fat one cut me off. "No, no, just sign here, here, here, and here," she said, pulling out pages seemingly at random. The gist of the forms was that I shouldn't reveal any secrets of tradecraft. Well, I never have.

Then I had an appointment with a doctor memorable for his atrocious drinker's nose, who spent a few minutes checking me over physically, then startled me with a question.

"Is there any history of mental illness in your family?" he said.

"I dunno, how about in yours?" I said back.

He laughed. "Oh, no, none at all. But you see, covert work attracts a very, well, <u>complicated</u> sort of mind. Such minds often break down under strain, under the very strain that they are driven to seek, like moths to the flame."

"Like Agent Freshleven?" I said, taking a flyer.

"Oh, yes, that poor man," he said. "Completely mad... oh, dear," he said, shaking an index finger at me, "I wonder if someone didn't ask you to see if you could get me to tell you things I shouldn't. Well, I can't: trade secrets, you know."

"I ain't that complicated," I said.

He looked at me real close for a minute. "Yes, you are," he said. "I see hidden depths. You know, I'm quite interested in what we can learn from people like you, people that can live a lie. If you don't mind, I have prepared a questionnaire, quite discrete, you understand. My own scientific interest, nothing in your personnel file. Would you be willing to —"

"Let's skip it and say we did," I said. "And the hernia test, too."

I can't imagine the normal process of induction into the Company was this cursory, but in a little over two hours including the wait, I was a secret agent in good standing. They gave me a limo ride back to Andrews, I was put on another chopper, and by four o'clock I was back at my desk in Norfolk. Two weeks later, I was on my assignment for the Company: attached as a liaison to Virginia Institute of Marine Sciences, to something named the Cetacean Intelligence Project.

That Monday I showed up at the Institute at eight fifteen. The breeze was blowing straight in from the ocean, washing away the great dismal stink. I waltzed past the MPs at the gate with my cover ID, a real life spook, a double agent already on my first day.

I made my way to the dolphin lab, and there in a patch of slanted sunlight by the edge of the pool, wearing one of those new bikini swimsuits, sat Caroline Lockwood, the head trainer. She was a knockout.

"Howdy, ma'am," I said. I was big on John Wayne.

She had squinty little eyes, almost like a Chinese girl, but dark blue. She squinted even harder as she looked me over.

"Who the hell are you?"

"My name's Charlie Marlow."

"What the hell are you doing in my lab, Charlie Marlow?"

"Miss," I said, knowing that she was married, "I can't tell you that. It's classified."

"Oh yeah?" she said. Then she whistled. A big gray tail popped out of the pool next to her and splashed a jet of saltwater that soaked me to the skin and ruined my best suit. When I cleared my eyes she was kneeling with her arms around the dolphin, laughing like crazy, and the dolphin right along with her making those clicks and buzzes they do.

"Charlie Marlow, meet Tatiana, dolphin number nine," she said, Chinese eyes smiling. "She's classified, too."

A sunburned man with a trimmed red beard and horn-rimmed sunglasses came through the office door onto the pool deck and greeted me.

"Hello, Mr. Marlow. Sorry about the mess." He shot the girl an irritated look. "I'm afraid our head trainer sometimes encourages bad behavior in the animals. I'm Jim Lockwood, the project manager; and that's my wife Caroline, the head trainer."

"We've met," I said. She just kept on laughing the whole time, and Tatiana right along with her.

I went inside with Dr. Lockwood to find a towel. Then, we sat in his office and reviewed my assignment to make sure both of us had the proper understanding. He had a big handsome desk facing the window out to the lab, and beyond that the gently rocking Bay, all the way to the horizon. When I proffered my credentials, he waved them aside. "No, no, Admiral Long told me you were coming. I guess- could you just tell me why the Navy needs an additional observer on the project?

I relied on my briefing. "Well, its coming up to the big test in May, isn't it? What's your perception of the project status?"

"Oh, we're coming along marvelously. It took a long time for anyone to listen to us, my wife and I, about the untapped potential of Cetacean intelligence. Search and rescue, fishery management, underwater resource location mapping, transporting supplies to and from underwater habitats, long distance communications- the possibilities are nearly endless."

"Yeah, but what sold the brass was submarines: am I right?"

After the removal of the missiles in Cuba, the biggest threat to America was the Soviet submarine. The brass had an abiding fear of a decapitation first strike, where a single submarine with cruise missiles could destroy Washington from 200 miles away with no warning at all. Our sonar emplacements were stationary, easily detectable, and subject to countermeasures.

Then Dr. Lockwood came forward with an inexpensive way to field dozens of undetectable, mobile, very sensitive sonar units to scour the coastline for enemy subs. That was his hook for funding. And the big brass swallowed it whole. So he and his wife had a grant at VIMS.

"Funding certainly picked up after my presentation at the Rand Corporation last year."

I jerked my head towards the waterfront view. "I'll say. Business looks great. But how's the product?"

His red face got redder. "Look, I don't need to justify myself to— whoever you are. I'm doing groundbreaking work here. Admiral Long himself--"

"Admiral long ain't the last word on the CIP, doc. That's what I'm here to tell you."

"He's quite right, you know, Jim," said a tall man in the doorway. He wore a seersucker suit and was fanning himself with his hat. "I don't believe we've met. I'm Frank Gore, from RAND. Let me take you around. Jim, please calm down, this is completely routine. I'll speak to you later," he said, shushing the man that was supposed to be his boss. I saw how things were.

"No hard feelings, Doc," I said as I stood up, and offered Lockwood my hand. Felt bad for him: getting cut out of your own baby can't feel good. He grunted something and nodded but didn't shake. I shrugged and followed Gore out.

"You'll have to forgive Jim, he's under a lot of pressure," Gore said as he showed me around. "He's a brilliant guy, but not a natural administrator."

The project was set up like this: Dr Lockwood headed the project, and handled administration and reporting to the brass. Mrs. Lockwood handled the dolphins. They had a handful of techs and grad students for miscellaneous tasks: to tabulate results, maintain the underwater AV system, feed the dolphins, and clean the pool. Gore explained things in a light chatter as we wandered around.

His tone changed when we came to the office furthest from the water. "And then there is Dr. Boguszusky, in charge of linguistics and symbolic logic experiments," said Gore. Somehow, he made it sound like garbage man.

My first look at the Director's target, I wasn't impressed. He was the kind of droopy-nosed, stoop-shouldered fellow who had no worries about his draft deferment, 'cause of his weak chest, flat feet, and adenoids. He looked my age, or just a bit older. He just sat there with his bushy hair and his BO, never looking up from the mountain range of punch-cards laid out in front of him. The biggest stack was two feet high. "Please don't interrupt me, Gore, I'm assembling the latest program, I've been working on this for eighteen hours."

Gore rolled his eyes. "Francis, I've brought a new colleague to meet you, Mr. Marlow from the Navy."

Bogus looked up at me, squinting from behind thick glasses. "What part of the Navy?" he said. "It's a big place."

"I'll leave you two to get acquainted," said Gore. "Mr. Marlow, I'd be delighted to take you to lunch: the Yorktown pub makes a delightful crab-cake this time of year. Francis you're welcome too -

oh, that's right, shellfish. Not Kosher. Too bad," he said, and as he strolled down the corridor I could hear him chuckling.

"So, do you and Dr. Gore work closely together?" I asked.

"He's an anti-Semitic bastard. So as little as possible, really," said Bogus.

"But he works for RAND, and it seems to me like they now about own this store," I said.

Bogus put down his glasses, carefully balancing them in the center of a midsized punch-card plateau, and rubbed his eyes with the heels of both hands. "I know. It's a damn shame. I wouldn't stay, but we're close, so damn close."

"To what?" I said.

He shrugged. "To Dr. Doolittle, if you like. To every fairy tale every written. To the Garden of Eden."

"What are you talking about?" I said.

"We're this close to speaking the language of another kind of animal," he said.

At lunch, Gore ate his crab cake with dainty bites. I had a martini and the soup.

"Is Dr. Boguszhuvsky crazy?" I asked him.

He put down his food. "In what way? In that he sees things that aren't there? No, Mr. Marlow, I'm afraid we all do that. Quite normal. No, Francis is merely a typical Jew: a pedant and a bore, and deeply mistaken. He thinks he's uncovering the underlying grammar of the language of the Cetacea; but it doesn't exist. What they've done is succeeded in training dolphins to wear radio collars, react to transmitted instructions, identify the sonar signatures, and issue the proper alarm calls. It is merely an adaptation of a natural suite of behaviors, alarm calls against sharks and killer whales, no more a language than the barking of a dog."

The man seemed completely relaxed; in my experience, that's the best time for straight answers. "So, Dr. Gore, you're aware of my role on the project?" I said.

He waved his fork from my head to toes. "You? Crew cut, combat medals from Indochina, leather jacket, PT-boat captain JFK impersonation act? You're right out of central casting for the guileless all-American boy." He laughed. "Ten to one you're a dirty spook: Naval Intelligence, all the way."

I was impressed. "So, what's your angle here, Dr. Gore?"

He washed down his crab-cake with the last of his glass of wine. "Well, let's see if you can follow this. What's Lockwood's goal, what's he training these dolphins to do?"

I thought about it. "They're for the detection of subs, prevention of nuclear attack."

He banged the table. "That's it, you said the word: prevention. Well, what's worth a pound of prevention?"

"A cure?"

"And I'm the cure," he said. "The Lockwoods and their pets are undertaking a difficult task: to develop a robust and flexible system of stimulus and response that can be learned by rote. The Jewish charlatan has convinced the woman he can actually talk to the dolphins; that the only way it can work will be if the animal could actually be made to understand. Very well; I'll believe that when pigs fly. But even assuming he were right, the best this gives us is a warning system: underwater dogs with ultrasonic barks. I can do better: I can give them a bite."

That's all he would say, directly, but I got the picture over the next several weeks snooping around the project. Gore had his own little lab area, and lockers full of equipment no one else had the key to. But locks are easy. Mr. and Mrs. Lockwood, and Bogus, were trying to make the dolphins into the perfect sonar fence. Dr. Gore's job was to make the dolphins sub-killers; was to extend the training, so the dolphins on command would swim alongside the target and issue one last, special call. Their call would trigger the 100 lbs of plastique stitched to their back behind the trailing edge of the dorsal fin, and blow themselves up.

The days passed pleasantly: snooping, reading, and getting a tan are three of my favorite things. Sometimes, while I pretended to read dossiers on the project, I looked out the window and watched Caroline train the animals in the sun. I made no real attempt to get to know Bogus better; there didn't seem to be much to know. The man worked eighteen hours a day, every day.

Over time, Caroline warmed up to me, maybe a little. I was out there on the deck with my shirt off and my eyes closed, not even pretending to work, when I felt someone in my light. "Move a little to your left, huh?" I said.

"That'll give you skin cancer, eventually," she said in her slightly husky voice.

"Oh, next you'll be telling me that smoking is bad for you, too."

"Why are you here? You make my husband very nervous."

I opened my eyes and looked up at her face, framed by a brilliant navy-blue sky with trace cirrus. "So you sure I make _him_ nervous? Caroline, I'm sorry, but like I told you before: it's a secret."

Tatiana made a long falling whistle, then a crashing slap of a splash, followed by a machine-gun chuckle. You'd think she was laughing at her trainer.

She frowned severely, then put her nose in the air. "Oh what rot. If I really cared to know anything about you, I'd know it in a day. You're just not interesting enough to make the effort."

"You change your mind, you just let me know," I replied, with all the dignity and bravado a shirtless man with soaked feet can muster.

She stormed off, but then one of Dr. Lockwood's grad student toady, a flabby pale fellow named Mason, came over and gave me the stink-eye. "You shouldn't be bothering Mrs. Lockwood," he said.

I looked him up and down. "Mason, you keep out of it, or I'm going to tell her how you drilled a hole in the bathroom wall to watch her change out of her swimsuit every night." He blanched, and scurried off.

One night, about a month in, the phone in my hotel rang around eight o'clock, and I picked it up.

"Whatcha doing over there, Marlow? Where's Boguzhuvsky?" said the Director.

"He's home in bed," I said. "I talked to him plenty; seems like a regular scientist type. Still too early to say if he's a pinko."

He snorted. "You'll find out tomorrow, huh? What kind of pathetic excuse for an Intelligence man are you? It never occurred to you that your assignment was to watch him not just nine to five, when it was convenient for you? I've a good mind to have you arrested right now, you commie faggot."

"Look here, Director--"

"You don't know who you're dealing with, here. You have any idea how slippery this guy is? If it's who I'm looking for, and he gets away again because of your incompetence, its straight to the big house for you, got it?" He hung up.

I took out my shoes, and my gun. I thought about going to the CIA with the whole story for a minute. The Director of the FBI was crazy: this was something that impacted national security, wasn't it? I needed to tell someone, right? But then I put on the shoes and holstered the gun, and went looking for Bogus. I think I mainly just liked having an excuse to hang around the dame. Bogus was asleep on his couch at home like I thought, anyway.

But the next day, I came round and made a better effort to understand what Bogus was about. He didn't mind explaining; he seemed starved for company. He showed me how his cards ran through pairs of sounds, making an associative array: one dolphin-call, one word or phoneme. He showed me exactly what Tatiana could do, too. He had it rigged like this: a water-proof poster-board in the water, where little pictures could be stuck to it. Then a mike in the pool to catch what noise the critter made, Bogus's computer programmed to flip through the cards till it found a match, and a tape recorder with Caroline's voice wired to a speaker out of the water to play us the associated word.

He put a picture of a mackerel on the board. Whistle-chirp went Tatiana; flip-flip-flip went the cards. And Caroline's delightful throaty voice said: "A snack."

I took a picture from the pile of images, and put it on the board. Squeak-squeak, flip-flip, and then Caroline's voice said, more primly: "Hotel class submarine, also known as Soviet Project 658."

Caroline had come out on deck too; I felt a tap on my shoulder. "Watch this," she said. She took a picture I couldn't see and dove into the water with it. This time, the clucks and buzzes went on for like half a minute, and the card deck flipped around for longer. Caroline had surfaced and sat perched on the edge of the pool, staring at me with big eager eyes. I guess she wanted to see if her pet impressed me. I closed my eyes to show nonchalance. But opened them fast when I heard what her voice said next, to make sure it came out of the speaker:

The earth was without form and void, and darkness was upon the face of the deep; and the Spirit of God was moving over the face of the waters.

"Oh, you're having me on!" I said. "Show me the picture," I demanded. Caroline's face was triumphant. She pulled out a large-print waterproof text of the first ten verses of the Book of Genesis.

I looked at Bogus. "You've got to be kidding me," I said.
He just shook his head.

The week came for the big demonstration, the proof of concept of the CIP. The brass had been flying in over the weekend, and the whole shebang was set for Tuesday afternoon. Caroline barged into my office at eight AM Monday morning. "Where'd they take her?" she said. At first I thought she looked worried; when I looked closer I saw that she looked really frightened.

I took my time answering, thinking things out.

"Who? Who's missing?"

She looked me in the eye, and from the look on her face I knew before she could answer. "OK, right, your prize pupil, dolphin number nine."

"Tatiana," she said. Her voice was taut.

"Why are you asking me?" I said.

"Because Jim swears he doesn't know, and Gore just smirked at me."

"What about Dr. Bogus?"

"He said I should ask you." She bit her lip. "He said you might know, because you're a spy. That's why I'm here."

I guess Bogus wasn't as asleep as I thought.

"Well, I'm not going to lie to you: I don't know either. But come with me, and we'll try and find out," I said.

I went down the hall and knocked on Dr. Lockwood's closed door. No one answered, but I heard voices when I put my ear to the crack.

She looked at me. "Jim said I had to leave him alone while they prepared for the test later today."

"What's the big test?" I said.

"Dolphins one through six are supposed to demonstrate the suite of commands we've trained them for, echolocation of vessels that meet the acoustical profile—"

"Was dolphin nine supposed to be part of the test?"

She shook her head. "No, that wasn't the plan, she's too valuable as an intermediary, training the other dolphins what we teach her. Jim agreed we shouldn't risk her."

"There's a risk to the animals?"

"No, just to her comfort and stability." I raised my eyebrow. "OK, the risk is the animals might try and escape. They'll be off-leash, out of any containment. Our research with Tatiana, with dolphin nine, has gone too far to risk interrupting."

"Well, maybe that was the plan, and it changed, or maybe that never was the plan, and they lied to you. Because it's obvious that someone, and I think you know who, has got your pet to take part in the demonstration today."

She nodded, eyes downcast. "I know that."

"So, look, someone's in there, I can hear them. Do you want me to barge in there, and make a huge scene?"

She looked up, and she was crying. "Yes," she said. I took a skeleton key out of my pocket and jimmied the lock. Her husband was on the phone, Gore with him, both speaking into the intercom built into his desk. "Yes, Admiral, the animals are in position on the north side of the harbor—" I heard Gore saying as we burst in.

"Where's Tatiana? Jim, what the hell is going on? You lied to me!" she burst out at her husband.

Lockwood turned beet red. "Marlow, of all the flaming nerve, how dare you barge in here?"

I shrugged. "She asked me to; she seemed kind of upset that someone was taking her prize specimen without asking."

Gore whistled loud, between his teeth. He had his left index finger on the mute button on the intercom. "Jim, I've been meaning to warn you: our erstwhile Naval Intelligence liaison is a suspected double agent. I've been contacted by the FBI."

"Caroline, don't worry, everything is under control," said Lockwood.

"Yeah, but whose?" she said, and walked out with me.

We spent rest of the day was a blur of motion, a series of fruitless sprints around Norfolk in my convertible, checking with various buddies around town to see if anyone knew where the test was, or had seen Caroline's lost dolphin. She didn't see the point.

"The test isn't this big, physical thing, Marlow," she said. "It's about communication. We just create a message, and they recognize the pattern and send us the appropriate response. They could be anywhere."

"They still have to make up the message, right? There need to be mocked-up subs for the dolphins to recognize: something like a tethered barge—".

She shook her head, and her mane lashed my face in the wind. "It could just be a microphone on a reel."

I thought about telling her then about Gore's extension of her work. But I couldn't see how that would help anything, so I didn't.

Nobody knew anything. So maybe she was right. But maybe the point was, we spent the whole day together. She got to calling me Charlie, and I could tell she appreciated the way I hustled. Her eyes were hard to read, especially squinting into the wind. But when the chips were down, she came to me for help. That meant something, and it seemed like we both knew it.

We came back to VIMS at four. Her husband was waiting in the parking lot, with Mason and some of his other favorite grad students. They looked happy. As we pulled up and Caroline stepped from my Mustang his grin wavered, but then he lifted a bunch of flowers, and reached down and took out a bottle from a bucket of ice-water.

"Darling!" he said. "We did it. The test was a complete success."

"When?" she said, brow puckered in confusion.

"This morning; that's why I couldn't talk then." He gave me a sour look. "Marlow, I don't know what you've been telling my wife, or where you get your information, but I'll thank you to leave us alone from now on."

He turned back to the girl. "Come on darling, we're celebrating; the whole project is taking a cruise on Admiral Long's yacht. The dolphins will all be back by the time we return. Everyone else is already on board!"

He put his arm around her, and she settled back into his embrace; maybe after a real short pause. They turned their backs and walked down to the pier where I could see the boat moored. I just watched them go.

Then Smith and Jones pulled up in a black sedan.

"Hiya, shorty," Smith said.

"You're in trouble," said Jones.

"Go away," I said.

"You better go secure the target. The Director wants you to bring him to us, tonight. We'll be waiting right here. Get him off the boat with you, walk him to the back of the parking lot, and we'll all have a nice little chat," said Smith.

"If I don't feel like it?" I said.

Jones leveled a revolver at me and smiled. "Fine with us,

sweety."

He meant it, I could tell. The Director's personal bully boys must have had quite a long leash. I wonder how many souls they did in, over the years. They came to a nasty end in Laos, I believe. Something about heroin. Anyway, I could tell I needed to bring them Bogus, or I'd end up in a box. So I turned my back on the gun and walked down to the boat, their chuckles in my ears.

At the boat gangway, they were already all aboard and pulling away. Mason didn't want to let me on. But Caroline saw me and waved. "Now Mason, be nice. Charlie, come on. It's OK, we talked and Jim explained the whole thing to me. And I told him how you just tried to help me. Come on Mason, get out of the way."

She pushed him aside, and gave me her hand and pulled me aboard as I jumped the gap. From the look on his face, I thought she ought to be more careful who she shoved.

The sunset was a fine dark red against the clouds, and the booze was flowing freely. They had a little band and after sundown the atmosphere was really festive, even though the wind was up and it got a little choppy. Admiral Long wasn't there himself, just his staff; Dr. Gore was playing host to assorted brass and some other suits from Rand. I found Bogus in corner at the back of the boat, and had a quiet chat.

"So what makes you think I'm a spy?" I asked him.

"Because you are," he said.

"So why'd you tell Caroline that I'd help her?"

He shrugged. "Because you're decent, deep down. I have a feel for these things."

After that I had had the choice to make a liar out of him, or tell him what was waiting for him back at VIMS. I chose to tell him the truth. It took a little while.

"Ah, if it isn't Charles and Francis, sitting like two little love-birds," said Gore, clapping his hand on my back.

I grabbed his wrist and bent it behind his back. "I'd watch myself Dr. Gore, if I was you," I said.

Gore grimaced. "Let me go right now or you're going to the stockade the minute this boat lands. He looked over at Bogus, who was stock still, taking it all in, probably still figuring out that he was somehow both at the top of the FBI Director's Most Wanted list, and was the object of the delusional attentions of the CIA's chief of

Counter-Intelligence.

"What are you looking at, big nose?" said Gore.

Bogus kind of came back to himself. He smiled a little, then walked up and slapped Gore across the face, just as I was letting him go. "Go fuck yourself, Gore," he said.

Well, Dr. Gore came at him with both hands flailing, and before I could grab him again Bogus fell back, and an unlucky swell made the boat pitch starboard a little and next thing I knew Bogus was over the side. My assignment, the Director's target, Angleton's Gerontion, was over the side.

"Man overboard!" I screamed. I was about to go in after him but Caroline ran up and stopped me. "Don't, it's real rough out there," she gasped.

I shook her off and jumped. I'm a fair swimmer. But it was choppy, and dark, and Bogus must've sunk like a stone. I didn't see a thing.

They stopped the boat and put up floodlights and tossed out all the life preservers. But they didn't find him either.

On the way back, I told her everything I knew about Gore and the CIP. When the boat landed, she ran off to the dolphin pens, to count the dolphins.

"There's only eight," she said, when she came back a minute later. "The others are back, but Tatiana is still missing. Where's dolphin number nine, Jim?" she said, her voice controlled but with a hint of hysteria.

He looked awful; no more champagne and roses this time. "Honey, there was— there was one additional test. I'm afraid," he said, and then trailed off.

"Yes?" she said, frozen.

"Tatiana, something happened and, well, she didn't make it. She's not coming back," he said.

She slapped him hard, real hard, and ran off; and instead of worrying about Smith and Jones I just ran after her. I don't think Lockwood chased her at all. Mason tried to stop me, but I socked him one and left him gasping in the mud. I caught up with her in a downpour and put my coat around her shoulders; and she kissed me. I tasted her tears through the rain. We went to my Mustang, I put the top up, and I ran a bunch of red lights on the way back to my place.

Well, I thought I'd be happier than I was to finally get into her pants. But the way it was, it really just made me pretty sad. I thought it through. There was no more Bogus, no more Tatiana, and no more marriage to Jim; so it seemed like there was no more reason for her to be there. Or me either. There was no possible future where we'd be together. I saw it all as we got ready to make love. But I didn't really care; at least enough to stop, I guess.

I woke up in the middle of the night alone, but saw someone in a ray of light through the cracked door to the hallway, fiddling with the chain on the door.

"Don't go," I said to her.

"I wouldn't dream of it," said Jones, and rushed me.

I woke up in a cell. I was on the bunk, with a bare mattress, and a single naked bulb was hanging from the ceiling.

"So you let him go, huh?" said the Director.

I rolled over. I saw J. Edgar Hoover, an old man even back then, wearing a black pin-striped suit sitting on an easy chair just outside the bars.

"Let who go?" I said, sitting up.

"The guy calling himself Boguzhuvsky," he said.

"Let him go? Nah, got some bad news, Director. He's dead. Drowned tonight."

He waved my comment aside as if I hadn't seen Bogus fall into the drink with my own two eyes.

"He ain't dead, son. Matter of fact, I'm not exactly sure that one's even capable of it."

"Capable of what?" I said.

"Dying," he said with a harsh chuckle. "That one, he's special. He's real old, and real special."

I saw no door or window or any other features of the room where I was. It seemed like I might be there a long time, maybe the rest of my life. I thought I might as well get a story while I waited.

"Director, you've been hinting about this guy from the beginning, but never told me anything. Want to give me a clue what you're talking about?" I said.

He just sat there in the gloom for a good long while. I'm not sure how long. They'd taken my watch, as well as my gun, belt, and shoes.

"Sure, why not?" he said after a long while. "Why not? You ain't gonna tell nobody," he said, and gave me a smile that poured ice down my spine. "It's pretty simple. Here's what I know: that Bogus fella- he can raise the dead."

I jerked my head up to stare at him, but he was looking so far into the past he couldn't see me anymore.

"Back in 1920, I was on a raid, with some boys kinda like Smith and Jones, here. In DC. I was born there, I'm not ashamed to say. The finest city in the world, ask anyone. During the Great War, I'd been working on Enemy Alien Registration, and I'd seen this fella's name come up, called himself Bertelsmann. He was a restaurateur, of no known nationality, rich as hell. Didn't pay taxes, had legal papers but shouldn't have.

"So we went in quiet at first, like customers. One of his people, a jazzman, gave me some lip, and I plugged him. Bertelsmann... Bogus... well, whoever he was, he just goes down and kneels over his friend for half a minute. Then, 'Praise Jesus, praise God almighty,' and up pops the spade, who I'd shot dead ten seconds before. Then he said it louder, and he started singing it. And some wiseacre in the band blew out the applause riff, and the crowd went nuts, and the old spade kept on singing hallelujah, and my boys turned white and ran for the door, and women were screaming and crying, and Bertelsmann was just shaking his head smiling at me.

"Something was funny, but I didn't know what, and I didn't know what to do; I couldn't stay there alone. I came back that night with a warrant and a posse. The place was boarded up and empty like there was never anything there except the heap of scrap metal we found when we busted down the door. So I went to the courthouse, and no one had any record of him, and I went back to my office to find my file, and it was missing too.

"So I let it drop, for then; but I was looking for him forever after. Nobody makes a fool of me. I had to know how it was done. If it was a fake, then I'd break his bones till he showed me the trick. If it was real, why then, I had all kinds of new questions for him. Nobody keeps secrets from J. Edgar Hoover."

So there I was, in the cell with this old man telling me stories, and already so much as told me I wasn't getting out of there alive. I still remember how scared I was, as I realized just how far the Director of the FBI was out of his god-damn mind. But I just couldn't help but smart-aleck a doozy like that.

"So, Director, are you looking for Jesus?"

His voice at the end was real soft. "Son, I just don't know."

"Well, you've found him," said a voice from the corner.

Hoover jumped like a much younger man, and screamed like a woman. "Who's there?" he yelled, and waved Smith and Jones forward.

They ran over, and ran back my belt, which was talking. "James Jesus Angleton, at your service, Director," said the voice from the hidden radio. "I'll be needing my agent back now, I think."

"Son of a bitch," said the Director. "Did neither one of you idiots think to search him for bugs?"

Smith and Jones looked so shame-faced I wished it could've been my idea. But I was more surprised than anyone to hear voices coming out of my clothing.

"Angleton, I don't know what you think you're about, here, but you are interfering in one of my investigations," said the Director.

"Your investigations. So successful they are, always. Like in Dallas," said Angleton. "Listen to me. Either you return my agent to the Ceteacean lab, unharmed, in one hour… or you'll be facing a Congressional hearing over your fitness for office on Thursday, on grounds of senility. I have your entire rambling anecdote on tape."

"Senile?" the Director roared. "Bullshit! You know as good as I do, this guy Bogus is a – well, anyway, you know he ain't normal."

"I'm afraid neither one of us will ever know now, thanks to your bungling, Hoover," said Angleton, sounding a little hot himself for the first time. "And if you don't think I can convince Congress you're senile, how do you like my chances of proving you're a homosexual?"

"Going that route, eh?" The Director chuckled, a sound like crumbling concrete. "Fine. You can have your boy. But I challenge you, Angleton, you Ivy-League piece of shit. You and all your fancy big ideas, you think you're so fucking smart. Listen to me. I will find my Bertelsmann, your Gerontion… I will find him again. And I will learn his secrets, and make them my own." He lifted his head. His eyes were a flame. "I'm an old man. And you're no spring chicken. So I say, lets meet up, fifty years from today, and discuss who's got the better investigatory methodology. How's that?" He laughed again, an ugly sound. "The winner gets to still be alive."

"You're on," said Angleton, after a pause. "The Yorktown Pub's been there for nearly a hundred years; I'm sure it'll last another fifty. Meet me in the Gentlemen's Lounge, anytime, any afternoon in the Spring 2015. I'll buy you a drink. Now release Mr. Marlow."

The Director leaned back and jerked his thumb at me over his shoulder, not even looking at me. "Sure thing, you'll get him. Smith, Jones, get this pretty boy out of here. I'm tired of him." The bruisers came back in, Smith smiled at me and Jones socked me and that's the last I ever saw of them or the Director.

The spook's story just trailed off into a silence that stretched on and on. I became aware of Headline Sports blaring about Game Six again, and realized half an hour had passed. Marlow sat upright but his eyes were down, maybe looking for something out of the past. He only found his drink.

"So what happened?" I said to Marlow.

He looked up startled, as if surprised to realize I was there, then shrugged.

"I dunno. I guess I worked for twenty five years fighting commies day and night, to wake up one spring to realize the USSR was dead as a doornail - and that I was old.

"No!"

He laughed. "Oh, I'm old enough all right, son."

"I mean, to the project, to Caroline and Dr. Gore: to the Cetacean Intelligence Project," I said.

"Oh, that," he said. "Well, I woke up back in my hotel around six the next morning, with a splitting headache. I went in to VIMS early, hoping to catch Caroline with no one else around.

"But there was police tape across the front door, and the MPs were out in force.

"Where were you last night?" said Angleton, materializing from a side-door. "Get in here, you: I need my message from Gerontion."

"What are you talking about?" I said.

"He called me last night. Told me where to find the receiver to the bug in your belt. Said if I kept you safe he'd make it worth my while."

I was flabbergasted. "So you didn't even keep me safe yourself?"

He shrugged. "You didn't tell me you were in with Hoover, you let Gerontion escape; why was I going to put myself out for you? But hey, I did my part, here you are, hardly worse for wear, just a bruise or two. So, where's my message?"

I shook my head. "What's going on out there?" I asked. "Tell me that first." I was starting to get a bad feeling, because while I didn't see an ambulance, I had just spotted a hearse."

Angleton shrugged again. "I don't really know— I think perhaps someone killed Dr. Gore."

"What?" I said. "How can you not know? Isn't it your job to know things like that?"

He looked a little embarrassed. "Well, I don't think it was the Russians," he said.

It took me half an hour to get into the lab, but they still were fishing a body out of the water, from pool number nine. A bunch of cops were standing at the edge with a pool skimmer. No one would get in the tank; they were afraid of the dolphins. One of the feet was all chewed up and bloody. But from his argyle sock on the other foot I knew it was Gore.

"Quick," said Angleton. "Where's the goods from Gerontion? I know this has been some ride for you Charlie, a helluva ride for your first rodeo, but this is the finish. Get me what I want, and I'll back you all the way. Come through, discretely, and you're CIA for life, and under my protection. Flub it and..." he shook his head. "I'm afraid it's back to the Navy for you. And I can't promise you any help with Hoover."

I thought and thought, pacing back and forth on the pool deck, trying to ignore the bumbling, tentative cops. Carolyn and Jim Lockwood were being interviewed by detectives in their separate offices. I felt her eyes on me once, and tried hard to make sense of what I saw in them; then the blind was drawn.

But I had it. "Get me into Bogus's office," I said. "You're message is in there."

He shook his head. "No dice, my people have already been through there with a fine toothed comb. There's nothing there but scientific equipment. Try again."

"It's on the punch-cards," I said. "What he was working on with dolphin number nine."

He grabbed me by the shoulder. "Let's go take a look," he said. I don't know what he said or showed to the cops at the door but they scattered out of his way like a bunch of bowling pins.

I put the cards in the reader like Bogus had showed me, and it ran flipping back and forth for a minute, and then the tape spoke.

"*I am Lazarus, come from the dead,*
Come back to tell you all, I shall tell you all," Bogus's voice said in a crackling and jerkily phrased voice cut and pasted into shape word by word as re-translated to English from Dolphin.

Angleton hit the pause button. "I was right. I knew it. That lad <u>was</u> Eliot's Gerontion. The biblical Lazarus, a secret immortal, with a circle of unusual friends: Mr. Silvero of the caressing hands, a great thief; Hakagwa, a Ronin who bowed among Titans; Madame de Tornquist, a gypsy seer; Fraulein von Kulp..." He tried to compose himself, but I saw the tears running down his face. "You're hired, Charlie," he said. "Now get out of here, I don't want you to ruin this for me. Like Mrs. Brown said, you never did have the proper appreciation for poetry."

The spook's story wound down as he finished his last drink. "The coroner said Gore was drowned. His skull and ribs were also crushed. The teeth-marks in his leg and multiple fractures were consistent with death by dolphin. They figured he'd been bitten and dragged in, and a dolphin, or dolphins, had repeatedly body-slammed him against the bottom of the pool.

"Dr. Lockwood lost funding when his subsequent demonstrations for the brass were total failures. Dolphin number nine, oh hell, Tatiana, was never duplicated.

"Caroline was never alone in a room with me after that night. I saw her that morning, and it was like nothing had ever happened between us. She barely even spoke to me. I guess she felt I took unfair advantage.

"Her and Lockwood split up, though. Last I heard, he was in Orlando, on the board of Sea World. And she was still researching dolphins, maybe in Greece. But that was years and years ago. Pass the bottle, will you?"

The Wild Turkey fifth was empty. I stretched out and reached for a new bottle from the shelf. "You want another one of those on the house?"

His eyes re-focused. "Nah, ring it up. I pay my way."

I put in the ticket, then reached for his glass. As I poured he spoke up again. "It's my last time in here. I retired today."

"Man, are you serious. Your friends didn't have a party for you?" I said.

"What friends?" he said.

"Huh. Well, where you headed?

"You know, I got nobody and nowhere to go, kid. But I am good and tired of the tidewater stink. Somewhere far."

I handed him his last drink, and after an appreciative swallow I asked him. I know it's impolite to question a storyteller, but I figured it was my last chance so I had to.

"Well, there's one thing I don't understand," I said. "Why did Bogus talk to you at all, tell you anything? And why'd you tell him the Director and Angleton were after him? And why'd the Director and Angleton even think you'd be able to find out anything about Bogus in the first place?"

"Why'd I warn Bogus? I like to think he was right about me, that I'm good, deep down."

"As for the rest…" He looked at me for a while, then half-smiled. "You ain't guessed it yet, have you? I guess I've been lying to you, a little. See, I got to know Bogus a better than I let on. Let me put it this way: remember what I told you Angleton said to me when we met?"

"Wait, are you changing your story? I thought you said every word you told me was true."

"I just left some things out. This is what he said, completely: 'Because living with your sainted mother is hard, when you're sixteen *and you've begun to realize you're thinking about other boys when you play with your cock.*'"

"Uh-- You're gay?"

His face was immobile and pale yellow in the bar lights, like an old statue or an idol's. "I never said I wasn't. I said I wasn't a Communist, and that's the truth. But I've done a few things with fellows. Back then, weren't ladies in the Navy. So, I was like that. Not queer, but, you know. I'd get some boys after me. Specially skinny boys, like Bogus. They liked me. Like Bogus did, too. I guess the Director knew that. Sure as shit Angleton did."

I didn't know what to say.

"Oh well. Old news. Back to the future. I told you I'd tell you about the Cold War, too, didn't I? Well, it's like this. The news doesn't know the half of it. Trust me, inside three years, no more such thing as the USSR. Too bad I don't know how to do anything else. The good news is, we won. Right?"

The first rule of bartending is never disagree with the customer. Especially drunks. And I was only just realizing how drunk the cold warrior must be.

"Right. Well, that's great."

"Yeah. But we been leaning into the wind so long, when it stops we're going to fall flat on our faces. We did shit. Built the highways and the airports, put a man on the moon. Hell, we learned how to talk to freaking dolphins. Without the Commies, though: the guys with green eyeshades will be back in charge. They won't see a percentage in doing any of that."

He drained his drink. "You know what? The hell with it, kid- I'm retired. Good luck in the brave new world." He threw a wad of bills on the bar and stood up.

"So what are you going to do?" I said.

"Maybe I'm going to go find a dame who talks to dolphins," he said. He stood up, ramrod straight as when he came in despite the bourbon, and walked out. That's the last I ever saw him.

In mid-September, a month after a man definitely not named Charlie Marlow told me his tale, the Matt Davidson Band played in the Hall on campus, then went slumming at the Pub afterwards.

My boss was thrilled. Me, not so much: watching Sharon flirt her way to the band's table from the corner of my eye as I was slammed deep in the weeds slinging drinks was no fun. Especially when she made a liar of herself by exiting on the star's arm at closing time, beaming with pride. The man was certainly closer to forty than twenty, is all I can say.

I sulked for a week. Then I re-enrolled in school for the fall term.

Even assuming you believe Marlow (I'll call him that since he gave me no other name) in every detail, I give zero credence to the mystical fantasies of Director Hoover. Marlow might have been making that up, but it's also easy to see in the rearview mirror of history how a man who we now know was a twice-self-hating gay octoroon, who nonetheless rose to demi-dictator, might trust his instincts right over the cliffs of insanity. And I've read up on

Angleton: everyone seems to agree he was crazy, so much that 'Angletonian' is synonymous with arcane paranoia in the Intelligence world.

And Boguszhuvsky, if he existed, was no more than a brilliant mind who achieved before his time something I've spent my whole career attempting to duplicate. There's been some very interesting work. But no cetacean's have been found to have a vocabulary of thousands of words; there's been no proof of sentience. No dolphin I ever heard of can read the Bible, or write poetry.

I've looked for Caroline and Jim Lockwood my entire working career, asking after them, or people that answered to their description, at every conference and society symposium I ever been to. Nobody's ever heard of them. Not once.

So maybe Sharon was right after all, and the man who called himself Marlow was just a professional liar. But his fantasy, the promise that interspecies communication was not only possible but had already been done, a Nobel-worthy discovery just needing replication, was the lure that took me back to school and on to the rest of my life: graduation, my doctorate, marriage, children. It's a testament, if you will, to the beneficent magic of white lies, and stories.

Maybe deep down it's good that everyone so responded to drummed-up fears of communist revolution that we let labor unions negotiate fair wages, and we subsidized scientists to the extent we could put a man on the moon. Maybe it takes the existence of an outside enemy to create a feeling of solidarity and common brotherhood. Maybe believing in a lot of religious mumbo-jumbo makes people behave better and keeps them happier than they would be without it. So what if it's all bullshit? That's the considered opinion of my rational, conscious mind.

But what if it were all true? I guess I could go back to the Yorktown pub, the year after next, and wait around every afternoon to see if J. Edgar Hoover and James. J. Angleton show up.

Some days, I think I just might. Especially days after I have this recurring dream. I am not myself. I am Bogus, and Gerontion, and Lazarus-- a slight, dark man with a moustache. I've been called out of hiding in the night by an angry, weeping Caroline Lockwood. I take from her what she got from diving to the sunken wreck of a dummy Russian sub: the grisly jawbone of a large animal, studded with a hundred round peg teeth like soccer cleats. I carry the jaw with me to VIMS, to the aquatic mammal facility, and push open a tear in the chain link fence cut for me by the blonde woman in a wetsuit.

I get in the water, which makes it easy, when I close my eyes: easy to visualize myself descending, breaking the curved mirror of surface. I dive through sunlit kelp forests, past the warm upper depths where shafts of light shine on columns of bubbles, to the. I am going down deep, all the way to the reef at the twilight bottom.

There are all kinds of things living there. I'd call them fish, but that's not really what they are. I hold the jawbone like a dowsing rod, and it jerks straight and true at my target, one of the shimmering motes moving synchronized within an infinite school. The one I net is a perfect miniature dolphin.

We swam upwards quickly, past the big predatory things that aren't fish that hunt in the outskirts of the soul reef.

Then we are in moonlight, moving though swirling occlusion of kelp, and the underside of the mirror is just above us and we are breaking through the surface, beneath only the stars. For now we are we, and I am flying through the night astride 300 pounds of reborn aquatic mammal, which is leaping alive into the night of Chesapeake, rushing towards the Cetacean Intelligence Project bent on vengeance and liberation.

I am riding on Tatiana's back, resurrected and on her way to drag Dr. Gore into the pool by one of his wing-tips, then escape with me again into mystery. Dolphins can talk, God exists, the Bible stories are all true, there is magic in the world, and I am eternally living proof. And in that moment of realization, just before I wake up, I am overjoyed, but then really terrified.

SEX IN SPACE

I've jumped off an 80-foot cliff into the surf in Jamaica, still gulping my daiquiri on the way down. I've huddled behind the corpse of my camel as a helicopter gunship turned it into *Kibbeh*. And I've interviewed a man wearing a suicide bomber's vest. I'd be damned if I let Mitchell Wright, the once-pimply prince of the Susquehanna valley, face me down on a dare. He had the money, the power, and the looks: I couldn't let him have more guts than me, too.

"I'm in," I said. "But I don't get it. How can I possibly help?"

"There are still Soyuz stockpiles in private hands; they should still work. I know where to go, but I need you to talk them into it," he said.

Something didn't add up. "Why my help in particular?" I demanded. "Don't bullshit me, Mitch. You're a tycoon, and I'm just a photographer."

He gave a little chuckle. "Ok, I'll level with you. I need you in particular because Susie Greenberg always thought you were funny."

"Is it really you, Lou? Lewis Finkelstein? Gosh, it's so good to see you, it's been an eternity," she said, standing up from the restaurant table to kiss me on the cheek.

"Probably since 2009," I said, returning her hug and thinking back. "I was in London for the weekend and you invited me to a party full of crazy Russians at that flat in Notting Hill.

"Oh, yeah," she giggled. "You got so drunk you prepositioned my boss's married sister: everyone but me was horrified, until it turned out she was flattered."

"I'd never heard of a flight of different Vodkas before. Probably a bad idea to drink one," I admitted. "Wait a minute: why weren't you horrified, too?"

She crinkled up her freckled snub nose at me and winked. "Because at least you weren't propositioning me."

Susie Greenberg had been a friend in college too, who'd gone on to Wharton and vanished into the twilit and morally parched badlands of corporate careerism. I'd written her off for years: someone I used to be close with that I'd never have a meaningful conversation with again.

But there I was, sipping Dom Perignon with her at the finest table of a rooftop cafe, overlooking dusk upon Manhattan. Because Susie worked for Ivan Andreitch Von Koren, the oligarch. Von Koren, half entertainment tycoon, a quarter macro-pimp, an eighth biomedical entrepreneur, a rumored smidge of dodgy cybercriminal, and above all world class space enthusiast.

Von Koren, a Jew, but first a Russian. Not he, one of those Ashkenazi newly returned in armored convoys laden with anguish, weapons, and gold; back to the ancestral exile in the shtots and shtetls of their great-grandfathers from the fireball of Tel Aviv and fallout over Jerusalem, northbound refugees from the unthinkable that sent columns of surviving Jewry fleeing to all points of the compass, once again exiles, the Western Wall now half-buried in radioactive ashes, Jerusalem uninhabitable for ten thousand years.

Von Koren was in the original class of industrial bandits who absorbed into their personal holdings whole sectors of the USSR economy, swollen to titans in an instant. A whisper from a dying god was their bequest: "All my functions are now yours; for you the metallurgy of Norilsk-Nickel, for you the shipping of Archangel, for you the gas of Lyantoskoye field…"

Improbably, through degrees, first consulting, then doing work on his behalf in New York, at last coming in-house full time and moving to Moscow, Susie had become one of his chief lieutenants, the actuarial face he showed to Western businesses.

She showed it to me then, smoothing the crinkles out of her face until it was a mask of impersonal efficiency. "So, Lou," she continued, her voice gone from June to Siberian October in two sentences. "What have you got for me to show Ivan Andreitch?"

I took a deep breath, and concentrated on the fact that I was speaking to someone that once gave me a hug in the dorm hallway just because I looked sad. "Susie, you remember how I was in school - I used to just be your average happy-go-lucky technophile."

"Sure," she said, without thawing.

"Well, then the Second Depression hit, and they cancelled the Shuttle. And then China's property bubble crashed, they forgot about their plans for the moon. And suddenly no one was thinking about the future of manned spaceflight, or about the future in general."

"Someone's always thinking about the future, Lou; you just might not know who they are or what they're thinking," said Susie softly.

"Well, that's as may be. The ISS can't last, that's what they tell me. The air stinks, the wiring is bad, and it's a death-trap in the case of a micro-meteor impact. But it's still there. Its ugly but it still works, for now; kind of like civilization in general. And we're going, to show that people can still do it."

"Yes, Lou?"

"That's right. You read the papers. Since the Virgin Galactic crash that killed Branson, there's no operational orbital launch system. All the private sector white knights are off the board now, along with Uncle Sam, China, Europe – everybody except the Russians and their dwindling inventory of rusty Communist technology.

"Nevertheless, a few brave souls are going to blast off in a few months from the Baikonur Cosmodome in Khazakistan in sixty-year-old tin cans on top of 300-foot-tall tanks of RP-1 and liquid oxygen, to reach the half-shuttered orbiting space station, last of its kind."

"What tin cans are those, exactly, Lou?" she said.

"Von Koren's, of course. The 'memorabilia' that he keeps in

perfect working order in his compound in the Caucus," I said.

"You might want to ask people before you assume you can use their stuff. Now, what is it you plan to do with my boss' prize possessions?" said Susie, arching an eyebrow.

"What I'm talking about is demonstrating an economic case for humans in space. That's all it takes to turn it around. If there's money to be made, investors will sign up, new technologies will emerge, and hey presto: the dream lives."

"How?" she said. "What's the key?"

I took a deep breath. "The same as always: Sex. Sex in Space. Zero gravity, hot sex. Nobody's ever seen it before. People will pay to watch that."

She stared at me. "So, you are talking about becoming a pornographer? That's the reason for the trip, to make a porno?" said Susie. Her body language said "they don't pay me enough to deal with this shit." Her designer suit said "yes they do."

"Please, Susie, hear me out."

"All right, all right, Lou, I'm sorry. You just caught me off guard. Lay it on me. Hit me with your best shot," she said.

I tried to make my voice silky. "Here's the plan: I figure we get crew of attractive people up there on the ISS and do a whole reality TV series on them. We have the astronauts on the station walk them through the scientific aspects during the day, and we show flying fucks all night. People will tune in for that. So will every advertiser on the planet."

"Wow. So, I get it now. But I don't think people will stay tuned during the NASA channel sections; just for the night-time porn," said Susie.

"So we'll intersperse the sex and the tech unpredictably: you have to tune in all the time to catch them fucking," I said.

"You mean-"

"I mean one minute they're maneuvering cargo into the bay with a robotic arm on a boom, a guy and a gall, good looking, smart, classy: in space. It's the future. They're talking. We cut to footage of stars and the moon and planets, for mood. They're joking around, one thing leads to another... and the next minute they've clipped into some harness on a tether, clasped to the console, and they're going at it like nothing anyone has ever seen, literally bouncing off the walls and ceiling."

She stopped me again. "Lou, I'm sorry, but – why are you doing this?"

"The reason for the trip is to prevent civilization from making a mistake that will set it back a thousand years," I said. "In these times, the only way to get people to pay for spaceflight is to change the way they think about it."

"So you think the solution is to get people, get <u>men</u>, to think about Space with their dicks, huh?" she said.

"No. Well, yes, but… Jesus, Susie, if we as a society spent one percent of what we spend on pornography on spaceflight, there'd already be a colony on Mars. Don't act like porn is insignificant. People will buy sex anywhere, before anything else except food. I'm pretty confident Mr. Von Koren understands that."

"I'm pretty confident you know nothing about Ivan Andreitch except that he has rocket ships you want and that I work for him. It's pretty insulting, actually: I've seen better business proposals from undergraduates."

That stung. I looked deep in her hard hazel eyes for the girl I once (mistakenly) thought might relieve me of my virginity. "Susie, what I am proposing is something new under the sun: Sex In Space. It's a work of art, it's a scientific investigation, it's a philosophic, kinesiologic examination of a new way to make love, the act which makes us most essentially human."

I gave her my dirtiest smile. "And it'll be hot as hell. I am talking about creating the most lucrative pay-per-view event in the history of mankind."

She shook her head, fighting the smile I knew was lurking somewhere. "Lou, you're crazy. But I think Ivan Andreitch might, <u>might</u> just be interested in being a partner. I'm going to give him my recommendation that we proceed," she said, and with that I took one giant leap towards infamy.

I came out to meet Mitch in person to discuss my progress in the candidate selection two weeks later, a week after Susie let him know that Von Koren would indeed, with stipulations and conditions, give us access to four of his precious collection of Soyuz rockets.

Mitch had his limo pick me up from the airport and drop me off at his family's country house in the Adirondacks. Mitch was overjoyed and hyper, pulsing with energy. "I knew you could do it, champ.

She's always had a thing for you, you know. What a mitzvah," he said, slapping me on the back.

That morning I was in a good mood too, but still, ignorance must be resisted.

"No, she hasn't. And you know, Mitch, mitzvah means a commandment of God, not a blessing."

"Whatever; I think it fits either way. We're doing God's work here, don't you think?"

"You're unbearable. Do you want to talk about the candidates now?"

"Sure, sure; come on in. You hungry? Good, me too, we'll talk over breakfast, I'll get the cook to whip something up," he said, ushering me in.

Minutes later, I gave him my presentation over a medium-sized feast.

"I ran the advertisements in all the major feeds. The response was overwhelming."

"OK, let me see," Mitch said.

But he didn't like my picks. "No, no, this is all wrong," he told me after a few minutes of flipping through the stack of glossy 8 x 10s upside down to read each candidate's biography printed on the back.

"Mitch, you're not even looking at the pictures; come on, that's a good-looking crew."

He was silent for a moment; then he opened up on me. "I thought it was obvious. Where are the astronauts, Lou? Or at least Cosmonauts? What I wanted was adult science fiction. But you've got your phasers stuck on Porn."

"NASA shut down the manned spaceflight program a decade ago, most astronauts are over fifty at this point. They're going to look like shit on camera. I think if you're selling sex, you should select for sex appeal," I said.

He spilled coffee and caviar as he leapt up. "I'm selling the future. Sex is just the bait. Why do you think I'm doing this?"

"I don't know, Mitch, you tell me."

"Because this will work. This is the only chance for space in our time; maybe in any time. And we're going to give it up, because no one realized how cool it was. No one paid attention."

"Mitch, I agree with you, but --"

He held up a finger. "Ok, this is too important. If you think we have to, we'll do it your way. Get the lookers. But," he paused, perhaps drawing renewed strength from the slanting morning light, the flowers, from Spring itself, his dream not quite extinguished, "Just make sure they're smart, too. Sex in Space isn't a joke."

At that point, the phone rang. "That's funny, I don't give out this number," he said.

It rang and rang, until I told him to pick it up.

"Fine," he said with a shrug. "Yes, who is this? Oh. I see. Yes, Lewis and I were just – oh, he would? I don't think that's possible – ah. Imperative, eh? Very well. Don't come here; we'll meet you in New York. Goodbye till then."

"That was Susie?" I asked.

He made a sour face. "Von Koren demands that she get an equal say and veto on all decisions going forward, or no Soyuz."

"And you said yes?" I couldn't believe it, Mitch was never one to give up his prerogatives.

"What can I do, Lou? You see any other way this can happen? He's got the ships."

"Well, don't worry. Susie is actually still pretty cool," I said.

He gave me an appraising look. "Do you have any better clothes in your bags?" he asked.

"What the hell are you talking about, Mitch?"

"Look, I need any leverage I can get at this point. We're going shopping in New York. I want you looking sharp when you meet up with her again."

We had a ride, and we got a broadcaster. Mitch and Susie met at HBO's head office while I cruised Fifth Avenue with a personal shopping assistant. The meeting went well, apparently, once Susie gave them surety that the rocket ships were going to come through. They loved the idea. All that remained was to hash out the details. After much back and forth, they came up with the format: six shows, in space and on preparations on Earth, with footage starting today; they wanted us part of the show. I'd still be creative director, but they sent their own cameraman to start filming us immediately, a lunatic Yorkshireman named Martin Babbington.

"Good gig, yeah?" he said, pulverizing my hand as he followed me down the hall from my room, where he'd filmed me and my shopping assistant trying on then putting away my new clothes.

"So, what projects have you filmed before, Martin?" I said, still irritated that I'd been supplanted as lead camera.

"Babs. Call me Babs. I got me start inna nineties, kay, wif 'em Naughty Nurse School fings, right? Years One through Four. Did a bit of all right wif that," he said, then looked skyward and gave a reverent whistle.

"But then I got in wif the BBC, you know, doing a bit o' David Attenborough stuff, Life on Earth."

"Hold on, you worked on that?"

He nodded, grizzled face framed by wild strands of unruly grey hair, and cheerfully showed me a mouthful of rotten teeth. "Wouldn't guess I was a day over forty, wouldja? But yeah, I worked on that. Taught me a lot; 's where I really learned me trade. Went all over the bleeding planet for that, mate. They needed a bloke who'd go anywhere: bolted to the side of a mountain sewn into a sleeping bag for 72 hours, wif a bleeding coffee can to shit in, just to get shots of the nest of the greater spotted whatsit."

"You did that?"

He nodded. "Alwus been a good worker, hasn't I? Care about the craft. Not the subject: spotted whosit, galloping yellow-faced arsebird, piss on that. And on Nurse Bare and Henna Head-mistress: those stories was ballocks. But the pictures, mate: they gotta be right anyway. Images, patterns, details – 's a kind of Truth, really. Know what I mean?"

I in fact did. "I think we're going to get along just fine, Mr. Babbington."

"Babs," he said, reaching over and crushing my hand a second time, then raising his glass. "Goin ta be a pleasure. Here's to floating teats."

"To Sex in Space," I toasted back, and we drank.

I was the artistic director, Babs was the cinematographer, Susie/Von Koren was the final word on everything... and Mitch and I were at loggerheads. I guess I kind of flipped out when I heard that he was now one of the contestants on the show.

"What the fuck, Mitch?"

"Look, Lou, please calm down," he said.

"I am not going to fucking calm down. What kind of a sick narcissist are you? You think you can hire your college roommate to film you having sex in exotic locales? Forget it. I'm out."

He grabbed me by the shoulders and stared me in the face. "Lou. It's me. Mitch. Your friend. Your rich friend. I don't need you for that. I could hire people to film me having sex if I wanted; Academy Award winners, if I wanted. But I don't. So, why am I doing this now?"

"I have a few theories," I said. "Mid life crisis? Delusions of grandeur? Weird kinky fantasy life?"

"No," he said. "Lou, do I really look like a guy who enjoys the continuous search for process improvements which could lead to incremental increases in power plant operational efficiency?"

I got it then. No, he looked like the crazy son of a bitch who enjoyed flying so much he risked his life flying himself in a single engine plane every weekend, despite the fact he was abysmally bad at it.

"Lou, you are going to go up on a rocket. That's my gift to you, and I hope you appreciate it."

"Mitch, I… yeah, I do."

He nodded seriously. "You're welcome. Now, let me have this, please. This was HBO's idea, and I went with it, because this is how I get to go, the only way. So I'm going."

"All right, all right. I'll hide my eyes in your scenes, or get Babbington to film them, or something. Okay."

"So you're still on board?"

"Yeah."

"All right. Now let's go pick the other five."

"Five? I thought there was room for nine: three people per rocket, plus one rocket for the inflatable habitat we attach to the station to film in. Me and Babington are the crew. You're cast, that leaves six more slots."

He shook his head. "Uh-uh: Susie is coming too."

"Oh, no."

He smiled, and shook his head. "No, no, don't worry, little buddy: she's the Ice Queen, OK? The HBO execs really like that angle. She's there, part of the show, but sexually unavailable. They say it adds to the frisson, big time. Nah, don't worry."

"I wasn't worried," I lied.

We settled on the three candidates. Our first winner was

codenamed "Chocolate Way", a twenty-six year old black medical student and former All-American basketball player at Stanford.

In her interview, when Susie asked her point blank how well she thought she'd handle having sex with multiple partners on camera, she'd just shrugged her statuesque shoulders.

"Look, I liked to party in college. I'm sure lots of women, okay, most, would hate this. And hey, if it was a bunch of dirty old men, I would too. But," she said, rising half out of her chair to tap the photos of the finalist pool on display out on the table. That had been another of Susie's good ideas: full disclosure: to all would be participants, here's who the Sex in Space will be with, some subset of these people.

"These people are all <u>hot</u>. And I'm single, my parents are dead, and you just told me everyone will be screened for any kind of disease, as well as unattractive personalities?" this last to Susie, who again nodded.

"That's right, according to my best judgment." Susie had also claimed the right to veto any would be cast member on the grounds of being an asshole.

"Well then, it's Sex in Space for me," she said, winking at Mitch. Following his bombshell that he'd be one of the contestants, Susie required <u>that</u> needed to be disclosed to all the applicants as well.

It didn't seem to matter: we had serious applications by the hundreds, by the thousands.

"Let me put it like this," said our second choice, when we asked him about it. "Polaris", aka Dr Mark Loy, PhD in physics, was a fit forty year old Caucasian and the one actual former astronaut in our crew of six.

"Twenty years ago, NASA did a survey. What percentage of NASA scientists, not just astronauts, mind you, but including all of their researchers, would go on a one way mission to another planet? Meaning they'd go, knowing there was no fuel or supplies for them to come back. <u>Half</u> of them said they'd go. So, you see: people are willing to die for space and you're just asking people to fuck for it."

The fourth side of our sexagram was a young woman that got saddled with the ridiculous label of "Chang'e", for the Chinese myth of a woman from the moon. Angela Chang was from a Hong Kong expatriate family settled in Vancouver, she was a former math team captain and varsity volleyball striker who worked in computer modeling for HSBC bank. She was destined to be the most popular star of the show, from her Chinese fan base, if the tally of hits on the website meant anything. She didn't talk much, but she didn't have to. I agreed with China: she was undeniably sexy.

The selection of the final two candidates was taken out of our hands, according to Susie. Von Koren would pick them.

"That's ridiculous," said Mitch. "Who's he going to get?"

"Well, he does control half of Russian entertainment business and sex workers," said Susie. "I'm sure he can find some pretty girls for the show."

"Susie," I said, "It bothers me that you can say that without blinking. I mean, the guy's a flesh trader, and you know it. How can you work for him? How much money can you need?"

She looked at me as if from a great height, distant and cold. "That's none of your business, Lewis Finkelstein. But for your information, it has very little to do with money." She turned to Mitch. "In any case, the schedule needs to be moved up. Ivan Andreitch thinks we need to relocate our project to Russia now, to complete the preparations. To his compound, in fact: he wants to meet you."

Mitch never liked to be told what to do, but that private stash of Soyuz was the last bus off planet, and he knew it. "Alright," he said with an unconcealed frown.

"So, Susie, what's Von Koren like, anyway?" I asked.

"You'll see," she said.

"So it is, how do I say this, embarrassing? For you to film the sex?"

I looked up from the monitor into the face of a slight man of average height, with short thinning dark hair and they gray hooded eyes of a bureaucrat. But he wore a silk kimono of splendor: Chinese dragons of every color of the rainbow chased each-other across a field of pure black.

"Uh, Mr. Von Koren?"

"Please, please Ivan Andreitch. But my apologies, I did not mean to disturb the creative process," he said, nodding towards the mat over which two of our six participants, Chocolate Way and Polaris, were continuing to hone their technique at rotating copulation, suspended by wires.

I rubbed my eyes. "No, that's fine, Mr. - uh, Ivan Andreitch." He beamed. "They've been rehearsing for hours."

I raised my voice. "Chocolate, Polaris, you guys ready for a break?"

"If you say so," she said, giggling. If I was embarrassed, she was not in the least.

Embarrassed? Indeed I was, when Mitch had earlier stripped down and I had to film my old friend for the first time, as he cavorted with the two Russian women Von Koren had contributed to the mission: raven-haired Natalia and her blond counterpart Tatiana. Four women and two men seemed the right ratio for the cast, all agreed. They spoke good if strongly-accented English and seemed both bright and pleasant enough; but judging by the whirlwind mauling they inflicted on Mitch they were unquestionably sex professionals.

"Lewis, you look unhappy. Permit me to give you a short tour of my humble abode, as a diversion," Von Koren said. I didn't feel like it. However, he was our host, and Susie's employer, and the critical sponsor of our entire enterprise.

"Oh, OK," I said, levering myself out of the director's chair to follow him. He led me down the corridor, a breezeway connecting to another wing of the house.

"This is where I keep my art," he said as we approached. It was a mid-sized museum, without the guests. Silent alleys of sculptures, paintings, textiles on racks, ceramics on pedestals, fabulous jewels behind thick glass.

Despite myself, I grew fascinated. "Would you mind if I took a few pictures down here?" I asked. "This is fabulous stuff, might look good on the show," I said, in one of the many long hallways of his Dachau we'd traversed, this one lined with a 10th century central Asian bronze bestiary of long-evicted species, lions, wolves, and bison.

He shook his head. "No. My art, my home is private. As is what we are now to discuss, Lewis Finklestein," said Von Koren.

"Please, call me Lou," I said.

He smiled is grey mirthless smile. "Fair enough, Lou. So, I wonder if you would be so good as to answer a question for me?"

"I guess it depends on the question," I said after a moment.

His smile faded. "If it were why you sought to harass and discontent my employee?"

My professional instincts, honed over decades of interviewing troublesome, often dangerous newsmakers, clamored for cautious de-escalation and diplomacy. I didn't listen.

"If you were to ask me such a question, Ivan Andreitch, I would have to answer that I disliked seeing my -- disliked seeing Susie the lackey of a baud and mercenary adventurer."

He sucked in a breath, hissing through his teeth. "As bad as that," he sighed, shaking his head. "Sit," he said, gesturing at an ornate teak monstrosity. I shook my head and he shrugged and sat himself, leaning far back, boneless and relaxed. "You are a perceptive man, I think, Lou Finklestein. A journalist, a watcher, a ferret of secrets."

"I'm just a working stiff, Ivan Andreitch."

"For instance, you suspect I control the computer worm <u>Shanah</u>, and derive income by renting divisions of my stolen host of processors. Hmmm?"

He raised an inquisitive eyebrow, but I kept my trap shut.

"You certainly are aware, and this I suspect is near the heart of your objections to my person, that along with rock bands, film studios, advertising consortiums, and telecommunications networks, I also employ many thousand practitioners of the oldest profession."

"Does Susie know?" I burst out.

His eyes glittered in the track lighting. "My foremost business advisor, hw could she not?"

"I feel sick," I said, ignoring my every professional instinct advising prudence and circumspection.

"I don't blame you," he said. "Rabbi Judah Halevi said a thousand years ago that as the corpse of a man is more disturbing than that of an animal, so too the soul of a Jew gone bad is uglier and more foul than that of other men."

"That's racist," I said. He shrugged.

"Regardless, for most of my life, I was that bad Jew, not even a keeper of the letter of the <u>mitzvot</u> but a thoroughly wicked person. Yes, I bought and sold girls, and boys. Thousands of them. I had men killed. And though I stole and stole, my thought was ever for more."

"But, he said, "there came a day to reconsider, and I did. <u>Kol Nidre</u>, two months after the Immolation, I changed. Refugees were still arriving daily, in motor-pools that passed through Turkey or Jordan stopping only to bury those dead of radiation sickness, often running out of gas here in the Caucus."

I sat silent, remembering my own feelings in those times of helpless anger and despair.

"There were encampments in every town in those days: whole tent villages sprang up in the squares of every city. Whole settlements of families, men, women, and children, in tents made of sticks and rags to keep out the cold. On Kol Nidre, I felt strange. Food did not taste, women did not satisfy, gloating over my wealth did not warm me. I felt bitter cold. At last I left my house. I told my bodyguards to leave me, to remove themselves from my sight, and I wandered the streets alone, seeing all. As sorrow and shame tore me to ribbons, so I tore the silks from my body and smeared the dust of the road upon my head.

"I head the prayers from a large tent and came in, alone, in my rags and ashes. No one knew me. I sat in the synagogue, weeping. They passed the torah around the congregation, to book given to our people, for comfort. I touched the fringe of the wrapping, and I changed.

"It was like an electric shock. When the shock wore off, I felt ... calm. Quiet. I realized that the voice inside me, that all my life clamored for more, agitating, scheming, lusting: that voice was gone. In its place was a quiet so deep and calm I almost missed the new voice, the voice of the <u>Maggid Mesharim</u>. Almost.

"But all that night and the following Day of Atonement, I heard him. I fasted, and listened, and prayed, and asked, and was answered, and obeyed. And ever since that day, I have resumed my old life only in semblance. You still see opulence and great wealth in my home? It but serves a purpose: all is put in service. For the angel of Joseph Caro has now spoken to me as well, and told me what I must do.

"Yes?" I said, resisting the urge to edge away.

"Oh, yes," he said, smiling beatifically. "To lead the people of Israel to a new promised land, which none shall contest with us. I speak of course of the settlement and terra-formation of the planet Mars.

The night before we left, Von Koren convened a banquet to

commemorate.   It was beyond lavish: the single sturgeon centerpiece must have been ten feet long.

We went over the final plan of the show, such as it was: very loosely plotted. We had a week planned: a carefully edited lead in show of dramatic clips from the past few months was to be the first show, unfortunately including me trying on my new outfits the day I met Babs. That lead-in would be followed by six twenty-four hour live feeds from the station for the entire duration we were going there, performing, and returning home. A Soyuz holds three people, and the Cosmodome could only support a single launch per day, so our show would have a staggered start.

They'd have a shooting location of their own, a sealed compartment with heavy new semen filtration system they'd brought up so our show wouldn't foul the atmosphere for the cosmonauts on duty Laevsky and Samoylenko.

Three more people was no problem on an ISS configured to house six indefinitely, but eleven people would strain its life-support systems past the breaking point. So the first rocket would actually be unmanned and launched the day before Mitch, its payload an inflatable habitat of lightweight polymers. Docked to the station, that would be the headquarters and main set of <u>Sex in Space</u>, season one.

We'd planned a thorough tour of the station, and some space-fucks. A tricky shoot, the plan was to put couples TBD outside the station in a tethered emergency shelter, basically a large sealable see through plastic sac.   They'd screw inside the sack backlit by Earthshine, gleaming up all through and around them.

Once the plan review was completed, I turned my attention to the banquet, losing myself in salt fish, cream, sugars, and a torrent of spiced carbohydrates in all their delicious forms. When I finally looked up, my stomach straining my shirtfront, I saw that mountain of delicacies remained essentially untouched. "Who's going to eat the rest of this?" I asked Susie, counting just her, me, Mitch, our constellation of tech-savvy eye-candy, and Von Koren himself.

"Ivan Andreitch is holding an all-hands meeting for his entire headquarters staff once we've finished," she said.

But the troupe that filed in as we left for an early bedtime seemed an unlikely fit as the retinue of our twenty-first century Russian prince. For one thing, almost all of them wore <u>kippa</u>.

The journey on the overnight train to Kazakhstan was a sleepless interlude of incessant tea-spilling lurches and anxiety. Through my greasy window I kept silent watch, as the passing scrublands ever dwindled in fertility, as the light failed and the moon rose and set over distant peaks of naked rock, till the first rays of dawn revealed the barren, ancient salt-flat of our destination, the Yuri Gagarin Cosmodome at Bikonur.

The Cosmodome was built on a titanic scale; such a vastness amid a vaster surrounding desert, a facility so extensible to be worthy of the Future wherein a dozen starships might call to port. A rocket already stood on the launch-pad, a green-grey bulk the size of a thirty-story building.

The pit surrounding the launch-pad was like an inverted Babylonian pyramid, right-angle steps of blasted rock each a hundred feet high descending into the Earth. The Cosmodome was the bittersweet and now all-but-abandoned fruit of an ultimately failed marriage: between the otherworldly ambition of the revolutionary and the world-class pragmatism of the Russian, survivor of the depredations of Hitler and Stalin alike.

We went through three days of rehearsals. Original designs of the Soyuz included a mechanical throttle and navigation controls routed to a joystick set in the commander's acceleration couch. Should something go wrong, had been theoretically possible for the crew to detect that fact, hit the manual override, and pursue their own destiny, the hands of one man guiding seven million pounds of thrust.

Modern design took that out. "Look," said a grizzled engineer with a bulbous red nose testifying to decades of vodka, one of our coaches for the week. "That switch was always of primarily psychological benefit. Even in the hands of a trained cosmonaut manual control would be of dubious efficacy - and worse than useless for passengers such as yourselves."

"Sez you," muttered Polaris, hunched forward in one of the slant-top desks of the briefing room, left over from the communist era.

He might feel capable of self-determination, but I felt it was all in the lap of the gods. I tried to drown my anxiety in more immediate concerns like picking and preparing our equipment for the shoot.

Courtesy of HBO, Babs had a never-ending array of high end equipment trucked in from Kiev in two 18 wheelers. I'd have loved to bring it all, but our cargo mass and bulk allowances were highly restricted.

We'd also have access to all the legacy cameras built up over a generation in space: the two man skeleton crew Laevsky and Samoylenko had shown us their inventory on video, including some dusty analog cameras from the early days of the station that hadn't been touched in decades. We settled on three high end digital video cameras for action scenes, and my sweet old Nikon D3X for exterior stills (for marketing materials and change of subject contrast). For his sidearm Babs chose a Fuji FinePix 3D. "Can't beat cunt in 3D, mate, it looks real enough to eat!"

Sunday was the first launch. I felt liberating reversal as I filmed Babs walk up the ramp with the ground-team to be strapped into an acceleration couch. "Good luck, Mr. Big," I said as I filmed Mitch coming next, walking past me up the ramp into the looming ship. He nodded his helmet, but if he said anything back I didn't hear it. Last in line came Tatiana, who as I saw when zooming in through the tinted faceplate of her helmet looked like a million bucks, a Sci-Fi cover illustration to judge and buy a book for.

I really considered the possibility that Mitch was right, that re-branding space travel as sexy was all that was required to open the minds and wallets of the rulers of our often miserable planet, and convince them like Pharaoh to let us leave.

With our travelers inside, I went scrambling back to my film trailer. I just about got everything booted up and locked in time for liftoff. Liftoff: when the pressure of the baby sun birthed in that giant's stairwell underneath made the green-grey tower shudder and then rise, slowly at first, incandescent engines gimbaling back and forth, bells of fire whose roaring toll was magically loud, impossible to describe.

For the close-up I used the cameras mounted on the side, in the shadow of the rocket itself so to save their retinae from the engines' burn, looking down through smoke rings vibrating in time with that impossible sound. Then came the moment of perspective shift, back to cameras on the ground, switching from one to another in sequence to capture the phases when the flying tower became the size of a plane, then a bird, then a speck, and then gone, only the plume of smoke left, arcing past the horizon to mark where a man-made object had left the world.

The first night was a tremendous success. I watched the show, and it looked great; Babs was a genius. Riefenstahl had nothing on him, the intensity of the images was electric. So were the ratings: HBO was already clamoring for Susie and Mitch to sign a contract for a sequel.

"Hah," he said with a wide smile for me on the video-conferencing screen. "Negotiate now, while the show is still just getting started? I think not. Who do these guys think they're dealing with?"

"You did it," I told Mitch. "I'm genuinely proud of you." And I was -- he'd held up well, for a first-time porn star. There'd been a couple of minutes that first night where he had trouble sustaining an erection (the problem was low gravity, he insisted to me, one hundred percent physiological), but Tatiana with the endless patience of a professional eventually got him in the saddle and put him through his paces.

The second day, the inflation of the habitat bubble went off without a hitch, and so did the orgy that night. The ratings doubled again. Everything was going exactly to plan until I got there.

My first problem was space-sickness. I was all tensed up, exactly what they tell you not to do. And the g-force was consequently rough on me, straining something in my neck and involuntarily voiding my bladder, so the initial relief from the crushing pressure of acceleration was wonderful. But inside of three minutes in space, I was retching uncontrollably.

After consulting by radio with Chocolate, our doctor, Susie gave me something for nausea that really knocked me for a loop. I don't remember much except her periodically coming back to my seat to check on me. I strapped back in though it didn't help, while Susie and Natalia cavorted in weightlessness, soaring like wingless angels. And I was supposed to be filming and I knew it, but I just couldn't quit convulsing enough to see straight, to tell if something was out of focus or even to point a camera. I was a mess.

"Lou, are you going to be OK?" asked Susie, her face pleasantly flushed with excitement. Now, looks-wise she wasn't a patch on Natalia, but at that moment Susie was the only face I wanted to see.

"I've got to take some pictures," I moaned. "Can you help — Grunch, ahhh, sorry, get my camera out for me?"

"What, so you can cover it with vomit, too?" she said, smiling despite some stray drops of my spew collecting in her hair. "Nah, don't worry about it, Lou. Try to sleep it off, OK?"

"You know what, Susie? You're very nurturing for a ruthless capitalist," I said. "How'd that happen?"

She looked happy, and then sad. "My mom was a nurse," she said. "Always used to take care of me when I was sick.

I used to want to be just like her." Tears don't fall in zero gee, they just build up until your eyes are basically underwater. That's how it worked for Susie, anyway.

I convulsed again, but managed to keep my mouth covered. "What happened to your Mom, Susie?" I croaked.

She just stared at me for a while, accumulating her weightless tears with nowhere to fall. "Lou, she was in Tel-Aviv, with my Dad and my sister," she said.

I barfed again. "Oh Lou, she said, patting my head gently. "Keep your eyes closed for now, until you adjust. Try to get some sleep."

I didn't manage that, but I did fall into a nightmarish state of fugue for the next twelve hours. I tried to have a meeting with Babs to discuss how we were going to split up the camerawork responsibilities, until he laughed in my face. "No offense, squire, but yus 'eaving a bit, aint'cha? Not quite right, you knows, for workin'. Why not wait a bit, eh? I got this lot wrapped up tight."

I wanted to at least observe what he was doing, form some critical opinion, do something productive – but the least movement, of me or anybody else, drove my inner ear psychotic. I went through the airlock to the bubble-habitat to try and watch one of the sex scenes, involving Polaris, Chang'e, and Mitch, but the sight of human copulation forced fresh bile from what I'd thought was an absolutely void gut, and led to curses, a break in shooting while they tried to mop up the gunk, and an ejection from the sex-sphere. "Jesus, Lou, take care of yourself, OK?" asked an exasperated Mitch as I fumbled ineffectually at the hatch, trying to comply.

"Lou, take my hand, said Susie. "Come with me now, that's it."

During the break I caused, and while Susie was trying to find the anti-nausea injection Chocolate had prepared for me, Babs decided to suit up and go outside. He went out the air-lock with a hand-held camera, to get footage of the scene through the port-hole, alternating with shots of the exterior of the station back-dropped against the Earth, to help the viewers at home understand exactly what was going on.

So he, Susie, and I were outside the habitat when the micro-meteorite punctured it. Perhaps the wreckage of an obsolete cell-phone relay satellite, the debris might not have massed more than a few hundred grams. But at twenty thousand miles per hour relative to the station, which it missed or I wouldn't be telling you this, and the tethered bubble, which it hit, it was absolutely lethal.

An entire hemisphere of the skin just melted away from the heat of impact, and Mitch Wright, Mark Loy, Deirdre Collins, Angela Chang, Natalia Zalabowski, and Tatiana (she had had her name legally changed so she had only one, like a Brazilian soccer player) lost their lives. I'm not going to dishonor their memories with those stupid codenames. One of Babs' cameras survived the impact, and captured the whole thing. Mitch was killed instantly, head pierced by a shard of metal, in the midst of fulfilling his dream. He never knew what hit him and I'm glad of that. Loy and Collins kept their heads and got two of the emergency bubbles open, and might have saved themselves, but died trying to corral the others into the waiting bags. They all died horribly, of hemorrhage and suffocation and I'm very sorry for that. I'll never watch that recording. But quick or slow, dead is dead and that was that.

But the show did go on. Babs lost his tether when the bubble melted, but not his head. He kept right on shooting, and started in with a calm and factually precise narration. He discussed his location with Laevsky and Samoylenko, but accepted it with resignation when they haltingly informed him they had no means of coming out to rescue him.

"Right, I mucked up the job," he said. "Should have tethered to the main station too, 's me own fault. Appreciate the thought."

He didn't say much, after that. Just floated in an orbit all his own, an almost unintelligible but implacable genius to the end, taking footage that to this day is legendary; the footage that gave

<u>Sex in Space</u> the critical acclaim to go with its notorious popularity, a show that combined unbelievable visuals with heartbreak and drama and good raw sex and adventure and technology, the popularity that has enabled Von Koren this year to extend the series to a still-profitable "Sex In Space XVIII: Return to the Black Hole".

At times Babs put the camera to his faceplate, so you could see him in profile. He was both crying and smiling. Somewhere above the Horn of Africa he ran out of air; you can tell because the picture quality suffers after that: he tried to secure the camera as best he could but his inevitable struggle to breathe at the end imparted a gentle spin. But the spin also allows you to see the station off behind him, if you blow up the magnification: first the wrinkled brown highlands of Ethiopia, then the station; then white clouds swirling over the Indian Ocean, then the faint blinking lights of the station, and so on, till his camera finally ran out of power.

At the time, though, Susie and I could foresee the lawsuits and the funerals and the slanderous editorials, but not the <u>Palm de Cannes</u>, Von Koren's immensely lucrative if decreasingly artistic continuation of the franchise, or marriage and the birth of our child. "We can't die, we can't. This needs to work," she said.

At some point I had stopped caring that I felt like hell, and after a while I stopped noticing, and after that I stopped feeling like hell. Plus, I had found some breath mints.

"Why can't we die?" I said. "Everybody does. And as for this working: well, I just went along to show Mitch I had the guts. I never thought this would go so far. But it's already worked.

"And we won't die now, don't worry. We'll take the capsule down, with Laevsky and Samoylenko. Just like two hundred people have before us, and thousands after us will."

I sat up. "Susie, tell me something. Are you really involved in a secret plot by displaced Israelis to colonize Mars?"

She stared at me, and I saw that look I realized I loved and that I continue to love, the one where Susie Greenberg Finklestein tries so very hard not to let the world know she feels like smiling. "Yes," she said.

"Count me in," I said, and kissed her. And you know what comes after that, of course, because we forgot all about Babs' cameras.

THE OH-SO-BRIEF RESURRECTION OF PHINEAS MCGOWAN

The rain intensifies as I reach the hilly suburban cemetery. I park and move closer in a different aisle, listening from behind a ridge. A chaplain and the few lonely mourners assembled turn up their collars against the damp chill.

"Mr. Boguszewski was a man of duty, and of strength. May he rest in the bosom of the Lord, God have Mercy on his soul. Amen."

He'll have to wait a while for this one. I need Mr. Boguszewski first. I watch as the coffin is lowered into the hole, and the man of God tosses the symbolic handful of dirt on top. That'll be it until five o'clock, when the workmen are assigned to fill this grave up. I looked at the schedule in the manager's office last night. I glance at my Rolex: four forty-five. I have plenty of time.

As the pathetic assembly breaks up and hurries to get out of the downpour, I stay inconspicuous, kneeling at the stone of Hyman Rosenthal, 1913-1975. I feign my interest: it's not him I've come to talk to.

As soon as the funeral party has passed me by, I go over to check out the open grave. Good, no need for a shovel this time. With a quick glance around, to make sure no one is looking, I hop right down into the hole, landing on the slippery curved coffin lid.

Rubbing my hands together, I close my eyes, focus, and do it. No, I'm not going to tell you how; it took me hundreds of years and probably cost me my soul to learn.

"Robert, wake up." He hears me; he's just too scared and disoriented to answer.

"Let me make this easy for you, Rob. You're alive."

I fumble with the latches and lift the lid, letting in light to hit those eyes that were never meant to see it ever again. Like they usually are, he's paralyzed with shock. But his eyes are open, and he's breathing. It's officially a miracle.

"What happened? Where am I? Who are you?"

All the usual questions, and like usual, I don't have time to explain.

"Listen, Robert, and look. See this? It's your coffin. You died. But I brought you back."

His eyes widen with fear. "Oh my God. I was dead. That blue car."

I nod. "That's right: a vehicle crashed into you and broke your neck. I read your obituary."

I look him in his watery, out-of-his mind eyes, and I ask him what I ask all of them.

"Robert Boguszewski, I have brought you back from the other side. I want you to swear on your life, which you owe solely to me, that you will obey me in my commands, and accept me as your master for the rest of your second life here on earth.

"I do not believe that you will find my service unpleasant. You are not to be my slave, but my knight. Will you accept my bargain, Robert? I have need of your skills."

His pudgy face takes on an expression I cannot read; the darkness coming quickly now.

"What skills exactly were you looking to me for?"

"Silence! Do you swear on your renewed life?"

"What if I don't?"

Distant thunder is my only answer.

"Well, maybe this is a dream, or maybe you're the Devil, but I think I'm alive, and used to be dead. I'll take your oath.

"I, Phineas McGowan, swear by my new life to serve--"

"What?" Surprise strikes me like a physical blow. "You're supposed to be Robert Boguszewski, physicist and military consultant."

"No, I'm just Phineas McGovern, accountant. Ah, what is your name, sir?"

That son-of-a-bitch bastard Boguszewski must have faked his own death. My mind races as I struggle to come to terms with the enormity of my mistake. But for once, while I decide what to do, I will make the time to explain.

He attempts to speak, but I cut him off, with a hand to his lips. I crouch over him in his coffin, in the grey twilight at the bottom of a soggy hole, and tell him.

"Phineas, my story starts in the Bible. People from Kansas to Korea have heard it; not just heard it, but pondered it, discussed it, lectured on it, and written about it. Preached it.

"But it was all an accident, because my sisters were spiritual and cute and happened to glom onto exactly the right guy. And they managed to catch his eye, became favorites of his. Especially Mary, who perhaps reminded the holy man of his mother.

"I think he loved her. Enough so that when their brother was sick, and Mary was upset, he noticed. Enough so that when she told him why she was crying, because her favorite brother, the one who sang silly songs and once made her a doll out of straw, was sick unto death, the prophet was moved to go to the village to cure him.

"Enough so that when he got there too late, slowed by his entourage, and my sister dared in her grief to observe that if he'd moved his ass when he'd said he would instead of posing for the crowd, her brother would still be alive… well, enough that it stung. Enough that Jesus wept.

"Enough that in order to get back in her good graces he went too far, and brought a dead man back to life. That man was me. My name is Lazarus."

I come back to myself, and listen to the rain, and the sputtering of Phineas.

"Ah, yes, hmmm… Well, Lazarus, I swear to obey your commands. Would you mind letting me up?"

"Phineas, I'm afraid I've wasted both of our time. Look, you seem like a nice guy."

He is barely able to stammer out an answer. "Y…yes, I'm a good man, Lazarus."

I slip my hand into my overcoat pocket.

"Good. So when you see Jesus, ask him if he's still sure it was a good idea to bring me back."

The gun barely makes a noise. Either does poor Phineas, with a brand new hole in his head. Christ, this one's going to cost me. But before the workmen come to complete the burial of the ostensible Robert Boguszewski, the coffin lid will be closed and sealed again, and I will have disappeared, leaving no evidence of the oh-so-brief resurrection of Phineas McGowen.

SMELL OVER IP

I made my pitch at Schlotsky's over pastrami sandwiches, mine without the bread because of an allergy. I always fill up on the free peanuts. "It's something that hasn't yet been done. We can be the Wright brothers of digital smell," I said.

JJ almost choked on his Cheetos. "Smell over IP – you heard it here first," he proclaimed. JJ is short for "Juan/John." He's maintained two identities, Juan Ortiz and John Ours, since before I met him in college, birth certificates and all. He's a brilliant cracker, stands five foot two in sneakers, and has the most balls of anyone I know.

"Let me pose a question: what exactly would be the point of digitizing scent?" said Kevin, who is all the things JJ isn't: sober, proper, responsible, respectful of intellectual property rights and other laws, and tall.

"Think about it," I insisted. "Sight and sound have been fully digitized, and touch is already being worked out, in medicine for remote surgery."

"And for military applications," broke in JJ. "Everything is ultimately for use by the national security apparatus."

"Yes, yes, JJ, the military-industrial complex, etcetera, etcetera. We know," said Kevin

"So, what do you guys think? You want in?" I said.

"To SMOIP? Sure, if it gets off the ground," said JJ. "It's an interesting problem, quantifying and encoding the whole sense of smell."

"The hardware's going to be our big problem," said Kevin. "Smell synthesis would require some really complex miniaturized chemistry. Storing samples of each molecule to be produced in a receiver would be very bulky. What you'd really want is the equivalent of a stem cell: a protein that can be transformed into others, whatever is demanded."

"Don't worry, I know a guy," I said. I took out a copy of the Stanford alumni magazine with Rajesh on the cover. The headline said: "Mapping Protein Configurations and Transformations through Distributed Computing."

"I used to take violin lessons with this guy when we were kids."

"Well, his wanting in on this is a sure thing, then," said Kevin, rolling his eyes.

Dr. Lulla loved the idea.

"I don't think I've heard a better grant proposal in years," he said. "It's just good, clean, fundamental science, in the classic tradition. Only by understanding and quantifying our human perceptions can we being to answer Spinoza's questions about the objective nature of reality—-"

"Great to hear you're on board, Doctor," I said, clapping him on the back. Rajesh always did run on. There was lots of necessary research here, years of it. He needed to get started.

I got my friend Sam lined up to do the business development. That basically means sales: lining up customers, expanding on existing business relationships, stuff like that.

"Sure, I'll sell it, if it exists. If it works," said Sam, husky and exuberant over our two-martini lunch at Champs. "I could sell non-existent tech, too; but I'd be taking on too much reputational risk, if it never panned out."

We hung out at JJ's crash pad in Ashburn, a decrepit old Victorian up a winding dirt drive off what used to be a sleepy country road, but was now a congested commuter thoroughfare. It was rumored that JJ kept another domicile, but nobody had seen it; we referred to it as the fortress of solitude.

The Pad, as we referred to it, was a barrel of fun. JJ didn't sleep much: he worked some nights tending bar at the Shark Club. Any day of the week, long after midnight, there was likely to be something happening at the Pad, whether J.J. was home or not. The bong was always loaded, and so were the delectable, giggling girls floating in the hot tub. We held a strip Pokémon tournament, played Doom and Civilization in equal measures, and generally had a fine old time.

But Kevin started drifting out of our social orbit. On one of his trips to China, he met a girl, a very respectable girl who'd been his contact/translator/minder. Within six months Ting Liu was working for herself and relocating to America, specifically Reston. Six months later Kevin announced their engagement, and two months after that they were married.

I soon realized Ting was a force of nature. Kevin's work went from excellent but laid back to brilliant and driven. As for herself, shortly after the wedding she quit working for VM and set up her own shop in direct competition, renting out programming talent to the same institutional clients.

One day after work, when she picked up Kevin in a Porsche, I asked her how she did it. She just shrugged. "I realized all the business model required was access to programmers on H1B visas. And that I had just attended a Chinese graduate school."

She and Kevin began a climb into the moneyed Tech elite, and JJ remained inscrutably solvent. But I was barely treading water. I made a decent salary, but spent all my money, weekends, and vacations chasing my dream of Smell Over IP. I'd taken this as far as it would go as a fly-by-night, part-time operation. I needed money. And before I sold my soul, I needed someone to draw up the contract.

Eric was a specialist in Telecom law and intellectual property, and a sometime friend, sometime rival from elementary school onward. I explained the whole thing to him at Morton's one night in December. "I'm confident," he told me over a bottle of wine which cost more than my suit, "that there will be big content providers who will eat this new communications channel up. Think, for instance, of the Food Network."

He cut a neat bite off his steak tartare, washed it down with a swish of the burgundy, and let the other shoe drop. "Provided you can pull this off."

I assured him that I could, and we spend the rest of the dinner going over the contracts, patent applications, nondisclosure agreements, and other individual snowflakes in the blizzard of paperwork whose chilling mass threatened to bury me. But I endured, and caught a cab for Dulles. It was only ten o'clock: if I caught the shuttle I could be in New York before Bill left the office.

Bill had been a good friend at school, but he was very different than me. We met at an allergy support group: me for my gluten sensitivity, him with severe nut allergies. We hit it off, but he traveled like a comet through my social orbit; he was always destined for Wall Street. Nowadays, he lived there, keeping an apartment in the city and only going home to his wife and kids Friday afternoons through Sunday nights.

I caught a cab from La Guardia, called on the way, and met Bill at his place of work. Heidelberg Partners, LLC: a mid-sized hedge fund running ten billion dollars of other people's money for the standard two and twenty: a flat two percent of assets managed per annum no matter what, plus twenty percent of the upside.

"Steiner," he boomed across the ultra-modern lobby of the Wall Street tower that housed Heidelberg Partners, like the spaceship in 2001 hung with abstract art. "What brings you to the City?"

"I have a business preposition for you, Bill," I said, and told him about SMOIP, how Rajesh had re-purposed his distributed computing processing-cycle-harvester to break down scent into a perceptual and molecular taxonomy. How JJ was coding right out of Rajesh's log file output, tailoring object classes and subclasses of scent to their newly discovered properties. How Sam was artfully drawing nibbles of interest from Vivid Video and other adult content providers, as well as perfume manufacturers. How Eric knew the trajectory of every sheet of the paper-storm, and how Kevin and Ting were tackling the problem of hardware, travelling off to Shanghai blueprints in hand. "Well, it sounds like you might really be on to something. Good for you. But I'm late for a date with a gorgeous martini and a refreshing blond. So let's cut to the chase. How much money are you looking for?"

I swallowed hard. "Forty or fifty million. See, the hardware components are really expensive to assemble, even in China, and --"

He cut me off. "Skip it. Yeah, we're in business. I'll send Eric the contract."

"Uh, I think I need to look at it first, negotiate over terms, maybe?"

He shook his granite chin from side to side, his self-assurance complete. "Nope. I'm giving you a hundred million dollars, so you're giving us everything we want. Don't worry," he said, raising a palm against my stumbling protest, "it's just the usual deal when we do angel investing. We get fifty percent of the profits, and all the patents."

"Bill, I don't think so. I'm sorry for taking your time," I said.

He smiled icily. "No, too late. You sold me: this is going to be big. I can't let you walk. If you do, I'll just cut you out, and do the deal without you. I know Eric: he'd sell out his momma for two million dollars. So, what will it be: get in on the win, or stand out in the cold?"

I gave the only answer I possibly could: "I'm in."

With the influx of money, everything happened fast. I quit my job immediately. Sam went into overdrive closing deals when the news of our funding spread. JJ said he had the whole scent palate mapped to his schema. Ting went to China with Kevin's circuit diagrams to direct some minions and fabricate a prototype. Rajesh said as soon as the device came back, we'd be ready for a test. Eric sent the bills, and Bill signed checks.

I started getting uneasy by spring. My excitement made it hard for me to sleep. "An opportunity for more research," I said to myself, and so I read, read, and read some more, always my cure for insomnia. But this time, what I read increasingly unnerved me.

"How is it possible," I asked Rajesh on our Skype video hookup, experiencing a stab of envy to see framed behind him, from my cold gray Sunday morning, his picture window into California's sun-drenched timelessness, "that there is so little modern research on human pheromones?"

He blinked in surprise. "Well, that's not really my field," he said.

"Of course not. But just hear me out. In the 1960s, behavioral science really started to take off. Researchers did dramatic, ethically questionable things like dosing unsuspecting subjects with hallucinogens and implanting electrodes in the brains of bulls so they could be made to charge and stop by remote radio control."

Rajesh gave an uneasy laugh. "Uh, where are you going with this?"

"Just two minutes, all right? Also in the 1960s, a Harvard

coed figured out that the menstrual cycles of all of her hall-mates, including herself, were synchronized. She hypothesized that human beings retained pheromone feedback and control systems prevalent in other mammals, such as those that prevent all but the dominant female in a wolf pack from coming into estrus."

"And?"

"Full stop. Forty years later, biology textbooks still mention the same anecdote, and no follow-up research."

"So I guess there was nothing much there."

"Or, maybe there was so much there that it all became classified."

"And our two minutes are up, I'm afraid."

"OK, bottom line: I think there is such a body of secret research on human pheromones and their potential for facilitating social control."

Dr. Lulla scowled. "Oh, that's ridiculous— secret bodies of science don't exist, sharing knowledge is the whole point of the enterprise."

"Oh, is it? How many journal articles on plutonium chain-reaction-triggering mechanisms have you ever seen published?"

"That's different."

"I'm telling you, someone out there knows a lot more about smell than they're saying."

We agreed to disagree. All keyed up, I drove over to JJ's.

"So what's cracking, JJ?" I asked him as we leaned back in our Adirondack chairs and looked out at the verdant April landscape on view from his deck.

"I've started a consultancy," he said, exhaling a cloud of smoke.

I waved it away. "What kind?"

"Intrusion and involuntary data acquisition."

I looked over at him, away from the sloping landscape of sycamore and oak coming into bud, dyed with Easter splashes of forsythia and redbud. "Defending against, you mean," I said, trying to read his swarthy face.

"You know what I mean," he said after a long pause while he finished the joint and flicked the nub over his porch rail into the creek below.

I thought of Kevin's probable reaction to this news; more importantly, of Ting's. And what about Eric: he'd wash his hands of

SMOIP if he heard this, he'd have to: with his client base any association with a felonious hacker would be the kiss of death to his career. And Sam had already told me about his low risk tolerance and... oh man, what about Bill?

I took a deep breath. "JJ," I began.

"Spare me, Steiner." He looked back at me, for the first time making eye contact. "SMOIP is your thing, not mine. This is more important to me. All of these stupid, arrogant, fat, racist corporate types are just begging for a takedown. They even pay me thousands upon thousands of dollars to do it to each other. It's beautiful. I think I've found my calling."

"JJ, I don't know what to say. I mean, you're going to end up in jail. Or in a box, depending on who you piss off."

"Nah," he said, looking out again into the wooded borderland between corporatist Northern Virginia and his domain. "I know what I'm doing. I stick to white collar macro-criminals like NGC and Lockheed. All they have to lose is other people's money: how much can they care, really? Now, I'd never go after a dictator's sequestered assets, say, or the narcos, people that know how to work with their hands."

"JJ, you are insane."

"No, I'm just confident. I'm better than them. Come on, you've seen the data-centers around the tech corridor! It's all Swiss cheese. The sys-admins have no clue. The day any one of those salaried slobs catches me, I deserve to get caught."

I spent the rest of that afternoon trying to change his mind, and reliving old times. Something told me it'd be a long time before I saw him again. Eventually, I gave up and accepted his resignation from SMell Over Internet Protocol, Inc.

The first demonstration was a total success. We invited a prominent freelance science reporter to our basement lab, in one of the anonymous but well-manicured office parks that have utterly conquered Fairfax county, the kind of place whose grounds could double as a golf course.

The writer, Dan Simon, was a real hipster: slim and tall, dressed in immaculate carpenters pants and a pressed alt-rock T-shirt.

"So, you can just sit right here, Mr. Simon. Please leave your coffee in the lobby, the scent can have a masking effect," said Kevin. "The device is an integrated synchronous sensory transmission system of sight, sound, and smell. Put your nose there, in the holster. Our team in Palo Alto (being Rajesh and a grad student), visible there onscreen, will send you a text with a list of five distinct odors that they will transmit to you in the next minute."

Simon's iPhone chimed. "Now, don't open it yet. Just sit back, close your eyes if you want, and write down what you smell. Ready, set, sniff," I said.

I craned my neck to see what he wrote down. Peppermint, gasoline, cut grass, Thanksgiving turkey, roses… and farts.

I frowned and looked over at Kevin, who shrugged his shoulders. "Hey, the email matches my list," the writer said. But what's up with that after-smell? That really bad fart-stink? Still a few bugs in the system, eh?"

We had Rajesh on a conference line. "Any comment, Dr. Lulla?" I said.

There was an indistinct mumble of conversation in the background, and then Rajesh got back on the mike. "Yes, I believe we have an explanation: my assistant George had tacos for lunch."

Kevin explained how the signal from the device wasn't just a snapshot, but a motion picture, reflecting changing scent traces in real time. Dan Simon's eyes widened, and I knew we'd hit a home run.

The next few months were the most exhilarating time of my life. We got a deal with Iridium, the satellite phone service provider with no profits but an enormous stable of satellites affording the only truly global coverage. They had a contract with the US Military, a bulk consumer of their service. I was proud of that one; I'd helped Sam sharpen his pitch.

"See, all these soldiers overseas, especially in combat, maybe back in the bush: what they want most is to phone home. Sometimes now they get video, too. But, smell is special. Smell gets you right in the nucleus amygdalae, the little parts of your brain right behind each nostril that are all tied up with memory and emotional reactions. Not just their voices, not just their faces: the smell of loved ones is the biggest gift you can give a hero; it's the next best thing to being home. It's tough to put a price on that, but studies show that it increases happiness, reduces mental illness, overall health, and productivity."

And so on. They ordered ten thousand units; their handsets were already huge, expensive, and indestructible: big enough to incorporate Kevin's transmission and receiver hardware, and strong and expensive enough to warrant the inclusion.

I went to galas, tech forums and mixers, conventions. Money was about to start pouring in to balance the volume flowing out. I felt a giddy tightness in my chest and an irrepressible propensity to smile that could only be pride.

Sam was the first one to get it. He called me in August from a flight back from the consumer electronics show in Vegas.

"Sam, you left already? It's only Thursday," I said.

"I'm done, man. I'm tendering my resignation as Director of business development," he said.

"What are you talking about?"

Sam broke a pained silence. "It's a personal situation… I need to spend more time with my family."

"Sam, we need you, you're part of my core team, a key part. Tell me how long you need off, we'll make this work for you."

He gave a bitter laugh. "I don't think you understand. This isn't my choice. I don't want to quit, but my wife — is making me. She caught me; she found out about Michelle, and Sharon. She got a detective; she's got photos, taped phone conversations, the whole nine yards. She told me if I ever want to see the kids again, I needed to drop everything and get my life together."

My heart wasn't in it but I gave it a shot. "Maybe this is for the best, Sam. Obviously, you haven't been happy."

"No. I love my kids; I have to fold on this one. His eyes looked past mine on the video screen, and stared into the middle distance, perhaps into the far-away country of home and family. "I don't know how she found out. I was careful. I mean really careful." He shook his head. "Oh well. I made my bed; now I got to lie in it. Good luck with SMOIP; an idea like that sells itself, you won't miss me."

Despite his assurances, I did miss him, badly. There was no smooth transition to a new head of business development. Sam knew the people, the places to go, and the lingua franca of the start-up scene.

I was still reading resumes two weeks later when Eric came into the office to see me. "Look at this one," I moaned. "He boasts about ten years of sales experience at a biotech firm that has never made a <u>dime</u> from the sale of anything. It's a black hole of angel investment. No wonder he wants a new job, but I'm willing to bet he's part of the problem. Why, oh why, couldn't Sam keep it in his pants?"

Eric didn't smile. "Steiner, we need to talk."

"Oh no," I said.

"I'm afraid there's a problem. I have a problem. My firm won't let me represent SMOIP Inc anymore. There's a conflict of interest."

"What does that even mean? Forget it; look, in two years this company is going to be bigger than your firm. Tell them to go to Hell."

A thin smile creased the tan face below his aquiline beak. "I love your confidence. And I really do think you've got a shot at something here, but…"

"But?"

He sighed. "Look, startups are a shot in the dark. It took me eight years to make partner, it might take me five more to get in somewhere else. I can't just walk. No offense, but I can't bet my career on SMOIP."

He meant won't; but I didn't quibble. What I did was call Bill from the prototype video-audio-scentio phone I'd decided belonged in my office, placing the call to the next-built copy he'd decided belonged in his.

"So, what can I do for you?" he said.

"I need a new salesman and a new lawyer."

He raised an eyebrow. "That's really more of a management issue – why are you bugging me? I'm just capital."

"I'd think you had a hundred million reasons to care if SMOIP Inc makes it."

He laughed in my face. "Oh, poor naïve Steiner. Man, do you not remember that Heidelberg Partners <u>owns the patents</u>? If you blow it, I'll just send in a pro to pick up the pieces and bring this thing properly to market."

I opened my mouth but nothing came out.

"Frankly, I am disappointed but unsurprised by what I'm hearing. Most start-ups founder under the weight of too many personal agendas and attachments. I've held off making a change for this long for the sake of old times back at school. But if you don't get this turned around soon, I'll be forced to consider alternative executives."

"Right," I said, and hung up. Suddenly, I missed Eric. I busted my hump to cover and find replacements for Sam and Eric. I worked eighteen-hour days and slept on the couch in the lobby every night. My big hope was the Iridium deal. Every great innovation just needs one high profile customer to popularize it. I figured in a matter of months, the irresistible narrative of the invention that could bring our boys in the field the very smell of the freedom they were fighting for would pave our way to the end of the rainbow.

I had almost convinced myself we were going to make it when Rajesh called me, so upset that at first I couldn't understand him.

"What did you say?" I asked.

"My department chair has initiated disciplinary hearings against me, I've been subpoenaed and questioned by the police, and they've empanelled a grand jury against me for grand larceny and fraud. My lawyer says I should expect to be indicted.

"Oh my God, I can't believe this," I said.

"I'm ruined. Carol's pregnant again, the twins are two, there's just no way I can take this. Even if I prevail in the trial, no one will want to give me grant money again, ever."

"Rajesh, what happened?"

"My old distributed-computing program, the one before SMOIP: it's been found to be an intrusive worm. It's been siphoning money from all the clients' owner's bank accounts to somewhere offshore."

"But it's not true," I said.

"It's impossible. Something's happened. I wrote that code myself. But someone's changed it. It's been doing what they claim."

"Oh," I said.

"I'm finished. That's the worst thing: my research will be discredited. My department chair will kick me out, the old man has always hated me, the senile, pompous fool—"

"Rajesh, get a hold of yourself. Help me think out what this means for SMOIP," I said.

"SMOIP? I don't care about that, man," he said. "I care about my job at Stanford, and staying out of prison."

"Rajesh --"

"I quit. I'd wish you luck, except I really wish I'd never met you. Someone did this to me because of you." Then he hung up.

SMOIP was ruined, too. Though the prototype existed, without Rajesh, there would be no Mark II. Dr. Lulla had been the indispensable man. And he'd been set up, no question about it.

I called Kevin, but Ting answered.

"Kevin can't speak to you right now, I'm sorry."

"This is a work emergency: I need to talk to my friend."

"I really am sorry," she said, displaying no trace of remorse, "but we are both withdrawing from your project."

"No. No, don't say that. Who got to you? What have you done with Kevin?"

"She didn't do anything," said Kevin after a pause. "I got an offer I couldn't refuse; I'm sorry, I have to quit, effective immediately. We're leaving for China, tonight."

"Oh. I get it," I said.

"I'm not sure you do, because I'm not sure I do myself. But I've been offered the directorship of a new technical institute if I moved to Shanghai, and threatened with arrest if I stayed by someone who represented they were from the NSA. I know which I'd prefer."

"I said I get it. Go. Go have kids — well, have a kid, anyway. I'll miss you."

As a logical person, I forced myself to consider the possibility that all of these defections were unrelated, and rejected it out of hand. The combination of sticks and carrots that had separated me from my carefully selected tribe was coordinated like the stalk of a herd of wildebeest by a pride of lions. I was now running alone and scared, acutely aware of the snarls closing from behind.

But this wildebeest still had horns, damn it.

I knew who to go for help: this was a job for JJ. I called and emailed, but there was no response. I gave him six hours; then I drove out to the Pad. I hadn't been since our argument, and from the looks of things neither had anyone else. The long dirt drive was beginning to be choked by sprouting weeds. There was abandoned, rain-soaked mail all over the front stoop, and no one answered the bell.

I ruined my loafers in the creek and suffered splinters in my hands to shimmy up one of the posts to the back deck. The hot tub's cover was off and was full of leaves; I felt a stab of desolation for good times long past. The door was locked, so I broke the glass, reached in to turn the bolt, and let myself in.

There was a note to me in the kitchen, spelled out in refrigerator magnets. "Gone to the fortress of solitude –Juan".

JJ knew I didn't know how to find his secret lair. But the name was a clue. Research in the old-fashioned paper phonebook helpfully propped up by the phone listed seventeen Juan Ortiz's among the million souls of Fairfax County. The eighth was him.

The fortress of solitude turned out to be an aging three-story brick apartment building on the border of Korea-town in Annandale. His was apartment 112, below ground under the front stairs. He checked me through the peep-hole, and then let me in with a grin.

"Sorry to not answer the calls, but cell phones all have GPS now; I can't afford anyone to track me," he said. "I knew you'd come looking for me, eventually."

"JJ, it's insane. It's like a movie, they're really after me. SMOIP is toast," I said.

"Thank God," he said. "I was afraid my strategy wouldn't work."

It came to me in a horrible flash. "It was you. You dropped a dime on Sean to his wife."

"Yes. He got nothing he didn't deserve thoroughly."

"And made trouble for Eric?"

"I barely had to do anything there. I think he was looking for an out already," said JJ.

"And ruined Rajesh? What've you got to say about that?"

"I thought you agreed with me, the guy's a pompous jerk," he replied.

"Well, this is for Kevin," I said, and I punched him in the eye, "and this is for me," and tried to kick him in the crotch. But he blocked my kick and kept hold of my leg, and then it was right back to freshman year in the dorm-room. We were rolling on the ground like two young mongrels, trying to establish who outranked who in the pack.

"Truce, Steiner, truce," he panted, after pinning both my arms. "I had to do it."

"I'm going to kill you," I said, calmly. "SMOIP was the best thing I'll ever do with my life."

"And it was going to turn people into mole rats, like ants," he said. "You were the one that taught me to always think of the big picture. Those receivers they were going to give the soldiers— did you not see what they were really for?"

"They're for letting them smell their families--" I started, but he cut me off.

"Bullshit. It was for hormone delivery, remote behavioral control of the troops in the field."

I considered the theory. And stopped struggling. "The Iridium mobile units were just the first deliverable, you know," I said. "We were going to put in home units too."

"And those would be great for pumping out signals for what people should buy. And who to vote for."

For the first time, I considered that perhaps I wasn't smarter than JJ after all. "You can let me go now. Truce accepted."

"Look, I'm really, really sorry. It just had to be done."

"But all you did was kick me out, and give the whole thing to Bill," I said.

"What are you talking about? Bill's just out his investment, SMOIP is broke, hey presto, game over."

"If you'd ever broken your capitalist cherry, you'd understand that it is an efficient system. People recycle. There's no way Bill lets this one drop. He owns all the patents."

"How does he own the patents?" demanded JJ. "That was never in any papers I signed.

"I guess Eric hid it in legalese," I admitted. "I didn't notice either."

"Oh," he said.

"JJ," I said, "have you considered the possibility that we're both just paranoid? How do you know, about those Iridium phones?"

"I know because I was in their data center, and saw the files myself. I saw exact specs for the aggression message, and another one for obedience."

"You know, I just might not believe you. That's stuff, if it even exits, it's so secret, there's no way it would be accessible from the outside."

He nodded. "Yeah, that's true. But I mean I went there myself. Juan Ortiz is a janitor, no hablo Ingles. No suit, sys-admin, or security guard in this day and age would ever suspect a toilet cleaner of looking in people's desks for written-down passwords, or of plugging in cables that were supposed to be unplugged. Racism judo, my friend, that's my trade secret. I can get away with murder."

I looked at him in awe. "But one of these days, aren't they going to see you on video tape?"

"Probably. But what did I tell you freshman year? My biggest fear is living too long."

"Oh, JJ."

"What're we going to do about Bill?"

"I have a plan," I said. We shook hands, and that's the last time I saw him. The next morning, I went back to ask some more questions, and the door was ajar. The apartment was now just bare walls.

I went to see the apartment superintendant. "What happened to the tenant in apartment 112?" I said.

Mr. Kim shook his head. "Very bad, very bad man. Sell drugs. Police come, last night. Take him to jail."

I looked back down the stairwell. I saw no sign of yellow tape. "Police? Are you sure?" I said. "What happened to all his stuff, the apartment's empty."

He stiffened. "You friend, of bad man?" he asked.

I couldn't say no, and got the door slammed in my face. Mr. Kim looked afraid.

I looked for JJ all day without success. I went down to the county police station, but they had no record of an arrest of a Juan Ortiz. Nor of John Ours. Nor was there any incident report involving the address. Nor did the State Police know anything, nor the FBI. I decided there was nothing I could do for now; I had bigger fish to fry. JJ would have to talk his way out of this one himself.

After dark I went back to my office. My card-key didn't work, but I knew a trick service door by the loading dock that smokers always left slightly propped. I talked the night guard in the lobby into letting me back into the suite, though he said he'd have to call his supervisor.

With no time to waste, I called Bill's office, where the second prototype had been installed. "Be there, you workaholic SOB," I whispered as I dialed. And Bill picked up the line.

"Hello, loser," he said. "Trespassing I see. Very well,

there's literally nothing you can do. Thanks for bringing this to me, by the way, this has turned into a very sweet deal. Lots of government contracts in the offering."

"Look, Bill, you know what they're planning, right? Basically mind control. You can't want that."

He looked scornful. "You know, this invention is great. I can smell waves of fear and failure pouring out of you. No, Steiner, I think this is exactly what society needs. People have gotten away from their roots. The alpha dog leads, the betas follow. That's the law of nature. Your invention just facilitates that."

He sniffed his armpit, then fanned his suit jacket towards me. "Here, this is what a winner smells like."

Waves of cologne and, yes, his stink, washed over me. I'm not gay, and Bill's a selfish bastard, but I got to admit: he smelled pretty good.

"Well," I said. "I guess there's nothing a loser like me could say to make you change your mind, forget this whole thing, suppress the research again, and shut the project down?"

He preened a little. "You know, I actually could. I got this one wrapped up pretty tight. But, like you said, why in the world would I?"

I took out the packet of Planters I'd picked up at the Seven-Eleven on the way to the office park. I opened it up, popped a few in my mouth, chewed them up, and breathed right into the receiver.

"What the — agghh. Oh my god," he moaned. "Peanuts!"

"That's right," I agreed. "Pretty tasty, for such a common food. It's a shame some people are allergic, don't you think?"

"Gurk," he said, clawing at his tie. "Ephedr—ough."

"Jeez, Bill, I almost forgot. You're actually one of those guys, who are allergic! You know what: if this technology spread, it would be a real pain for you. You'd never be safe; anyone who called could set off a life threatening reaction. How about that?"

He'd found his EpiPen, and was jabbing the skin of his neck with it. His purple color was already beginning to fade; looked like he'd make it.

"So, that's my pitch, Bill: forget everyone else, if you don't shut this down, you're signing your own death warrant. Have a nice day," I said cheerily, and hung up.

I heard the cops busting down the door to the suite. I could have run out the back. But as they struggled to get past my barricade, I just leaned back and finished my peanuts, with pride.

THE EYES OF A GENIUS

Despite the late afternoon Kansas sunshine that gilded everything it touched, the ophthalmologist's office looked a mess, of disordered files and discarded bags of McDonald's trash. Dr. Abrams scratched his elbows, then looked at the clock; it was four fifteen. He dug into the bottom desk drawer and poured himself two ounces of whisky.

"Here's mud in your eye, Albert," he said, and clinked his glass against a sealed jar of formaldehyde on his desk. The jar held a pair of human eyeballs, and a plastic label affixed to the glass read "The eyes of Albert Einstein (former patient)."

The phone rang.

"Abrams Ophthalmology, Dr. Henry Abrams speaking. How can I help you?"

As he spoke, he leafed through the nearest stack of paper, a series of letters from his ex-secretary demanding payment of overdue wages. His scanning eye caught the last page.

"Listen, Henry: if you think you can weasel out of paying me over eighteen hundred dollars, you're dead wrong. I'm now back with Ted: you remember, the boyfriend you told me to get rid of because he's in a motorcycle gang? At least he never gave me a social disease! That psoriasis you so repulsively scratch all the time? You need a competent doctor, you self-diagnosing drunk: you gave me scabies!

"But Ted recognized my symptoms and I'm better now. Anyway, Ted told me to tell you that if you don't pay me every cent of what you owe ($1,848.67), he and some of his buddies from the Pagans will come take it from you.

Sincerely, Mabel"

"Fuck!" he said, then, "No, not you, sir. I'm sorry, what were you saying?"

"I would like to discuss a business proposition with you this afternoon."

Henry tilted the blinds and looked down to the phone booth on the corner. He didn't see that idiot Ted, but someone was making a call and looking right at Henry's building. The figure wore a dark trench-coat. Henry let down the shade and felt for his keys.

"So you're a private dick, huh? Who hired you? Can't be Mabel, with those threads you must charge a hundred a day. I can see you right now; next time, use a phone booth farther away."

"I assure you I'm not a private detective, Dr. Abrams."

"You're from Carolina Medical Supply, looking to collect on their last couple of invoices. Or from the State Medical Board? You can tell me, it's OK. I'm a genius. I taught at Princeton. Dr. Albert Einstein was a friend and my patient."

"That's what I want to talk to you about."

Henry put the phone in the crook of his neck to dig in his lab coat pocket. When the rummaging fingers of his right hand touched metal, he smiled.

"But I don't want to talk to you," he said, and hung up. He took from his pocket a spray bottle of Cyclogyl. He picked the jar holding Einstein's eyes up and looked into them.

"Was it always this hard for you, too?"

If Ted (or the caller) trashed his office, he could always just give up private practice. He was pretty sure the Four Eyes at the mall would hire him: having Princeton on his resume was surely worth that much. There was only one thing here he'd miss.

"I better take you with me, Albert."

He wrapped the jar in a towel and put it in a cardboard box, which he taped up and secured under one arm. Then he rushed down the stairs, out the back door into the gravel parking lot, and trotted towards his car.

The thunderclap of engines and a shower of skidding gravel hit him together as one motorcycle cut him off from his car, and another from retreat to the building.

"Dr. Henry, you owe my girl some money," said Ted.

"Ted, that's between me and her."

"Not if I say it ain't!" Ted put his face right in Henry's, and gave him an ugly smile. "So, we can do this two ways, Dr. Henry."

"Let's do it the smart way," Henry said.

"I'm almost sorry, you scabby son of a bitch."

Henry reached into his pocket and touched metal. "Let me get out my checkbook."

"Uh-uh. You already wrote Mabel two bad checks. No sir, you give us cold hard cash. Till then, we'll take your car."

"You'll take this and like it," said Henry, and whipped out his aerosol bottle of Cyclogyl to spray in Ted's face.

"Aghh!"

Henry whipped around to spray the other biker, but realized the Pagan, a fat man with a forked beard in a Viking helmet, was wearing goggles. The bearded fat man hit him in the gut. Henry fell to his knees in the gravel.

Ted turned a tear-streaked face to Henry. "That was the smart way?" He socked Henry in the face. "Thor, give him a kicking while I wash out my eyes," Ted said, grabbing for a canteen.

Thor gave Henry a kick that loosened two teeth. How could he have known a biker would wear goggles? As the blows rained down from the fat god of thunder, Henry reflected on his life, a series of bold plans that never quite worked out. He'd modeled himself after the tough, smart heroes of <u>Astounding</u>: he looked at the world through the eyes of a genius.

He was a genius, close enough, anyway-- he'd taught at Princeton! He didn't deserve to end up here.

A gunshot stopped the beating. Henry peeped out of the fetal position to see the man with the dapper trench coat gripping a smoking pistol pointed at the sky.

"Get off him and beat it."

"Man, this ain't any of your business!" whined Ted, backed up by an emphatic series of jiggling, double-chinned nods from the Thor.

"Sir, these criminal morons were trying to rob me."

The stranger pushed back the brim of his hat.

"You two best skedaddle. Doc, you stay."

Ted took hold of his bike handles and then turned.

"Just fucking pay Mabel, OK?" said Ted. "You owe her eighteen hundred bucks, and she needs the money."

As the dismounted Pagans trudged off into the setting sun, Henry felt his age settle on him like the heavy parka he'd bought his first prairie winter. He was too old for this. Dodging creditors and private detectives, loving and leaving women, fighting bikers: too old for all of it. He'd spent his youth waiting for the future, for the gleaming rockets, the ray guns, and the sirens of the stars.

His youth was long gone. But the future, the one he'd been waiting for, had never arrived.

"I'm tired of life," he said.

"Everybody feels like that lying beaten up in the dust," said the stranger. "Let me give you a hand up. I've come for Einstein's eyes."

"No idea what you're talking about."

"Come off it. You left Princeton in 1958 when asked, after you refused to return Professor Einstein's eyes, which you got from the pathologist at the autopsy. You've kept them with you ever since."

Henry slumped, then nodded and took the proffered hand. "I've got them right here in this box."

"Oh?"

"You see, I've got financial - personal - ah, personal financial problems. And the eyes are the only valuable thing I own."

"Valuable?"

"When I look in those eyes I see the future; I'm the curator of a priceless relic, not a deadbeat."

"This is your lucky day, Henry. I'm here to redeem your custodianship. I need Einstein's eyes."

"Are you cloning him?"

"Look, how much money would it take to buy them?"

"No."

"I did just save your life."

"Nonetheless."

"Henry, you willing to just let me hold the jar for a minute? Promise I'll give it back."

"What are you going to do?"

"Just watch."

Henry always remembered the moment when the calm brown eyes of genius started looking back at him. Then somehow the man in the hat was wrapping a naked old man in his overcoat, and handing Henry an empty jar. The eyes were back on the face of a living Albert Einstein.

Henry felt a surge of such joy, that he'd not even realized he'd given up expecting to feel, that he feared for his heart.

"How?"

"Too hard to explain. I need to have a private talk with the professor now, but I'd like to pay you for the eyes. What'll you take?"

Henry opened his mouth to complain, to demand answers, to say he wanted to go to Callahan's tavern and have a round with Slippery Jim DeGritz, Gutboy Barrelhouse, Four-Gee Jennison, and John Carter of Mars. He felt, for one shining moment, that this was his big payoff, his pot of gold; that all his dreams could still come true.

"How about eighteen hundred bucks?" he said at last. "I owe a lady some money."

BROKEN MIRROR

The <u>Photon</u>'s sails are down. As I make my now-useless pass around Proxima Centauri, I can't catch its red dwarf winds. At thirty percent the speed of light, it took me twelve years to get here-- there will be no rescue. I wonder if Mom is still alive. Or Karen. No, not Karen, I can't think about her; there's no way for me to stay sane and do that. There's no such thing as Karen Dale.

But a Karen-sized hole in my memory is huge, a gaping void like the tear an asteroid just made in my light sail, destroying the nanotube fabric and my ability to get home. The continent-sized mirror of the sail assembly has been shattered, but fragments drift all around me. They reflect the running lights of my command module, winking as they rotate.

What was it that Borges said about mirrors: "Both mirrors and copulation are abominable, for they multiply the number of mankind?" Well, these broken mirrors are now multiplying me, and I have nothing better to do than look out into the abominable reflections.

Sex was another kind of mirror for me, a way to see myself differently, or for my father to see me at all.

"Gordon, you should see Hillary Park, my friend Joe Park's daughter. She's just your type, I really think you'd hit it off."

I looked up from my calculus problems on the tablet and blushed to my toes. "Dad-- Tell me you didn't say anything to her! Anyway, I don't have a type."

He clapped me on the back. "Are you kidding? Have you seen her Facebook page? Just fifteen, but tits out to here," he said, vibrating his palms an impossible distance from his chest.

"Nice, Dad. I swear to God, you leave me alone or I'm telling Mom you said that."

He just smiled at me. "Tell her what you want. But you're calling that Park girl in the next hour, or I'll set up your date myself."

I made the call, secretly glad to be forced to. Oh, I'd seen Hillary's homepage all right. That's why I was terrified of calling her; it meant too much.

I don't think sex meant that much to Dad. Or, that's not quite right. I mean, he played around on Mom, a lot, so he cared enough to seek it out. But he didn't seem to think it mattered as much as I did. Or Mom. Six months later, she came home early, saw him cheating with Mrs. Park through the bedroom window, and shot him through the glass.

I don't think I would have ended up anything special if she hadn't shot him. But it was another favor, in a sick way. It liberated me from having a family to keep me in the role of a child. I inherited millions once the probate court re-affirmed that a murderess widow is disqualified, and it gave me a damn good reason to work all the time: so I could never stop and feel.

College in Charlottesville, grad work at Caltech, and winner of a Pentagon fellowship at the ISS. I still remember that first liftoff, when I felt the elephant named Six Gees sit on my chest. I cried with release, because ten years of working twenty-hour days had paid off, and I was leaving the overheated, overcrowded, murderous planet Earth behind. And because I could at last once again feel my heart.

Back in the 30s, old Czar Putin single-handedly breathed life back into the decrepit enterprise of Western manned spaceflight, which had collapsed in a classic display of free-market failure. Even though venture capitalists could see no reason to fund human spaceflight, the mandarins of the People's Republic could. When the Russians realized the Chinese were serious about their exclusive ownership of the Moon, Russia became full partners with NASA and the European Space Agency. Putin saw the writing on the wall: first the moon, then its microwave-transmitted solar powering of the emerging bread-basket of Sino-Siberia; the next stop, total hegemony. To counter, the Czar poured all his country's resources into space, and dared and cajoled the rest of the world to join him.

So it was aboard a Gorbachev-class rocket that I arrived at the irregular cyclopean walls of jumbled rock and metal that was the truly International Space Station of the mid-twenty-first century. My ship-load made the tally three thousand people in orbit, a new record. Of course, there were ten thousand Chinese on the Moon.

At the airlock, I was met by a gorgeous woman in a skin-tight pressure suit, with her helmet under her arm. The suit was spectacularly painted, with an image that rang a bell.

"Hi, Gordon Jenkins, reporting for duty. Would you mind telling me what that painting is on your suit?"

"The Madonna of Port Lligat, by Salvador Dali," she replied.

Something clicked in my head, from when I still read for fun, from before Mom and Dad. "Uh, is that from Larry Niven?"

She broke into a warm smile. "Hey, you got it. I'm Karen Dale, Long Range Propulsion Project chief engineer. Are you the new narc?"

I felt another almost forgotten sensation: myself blushing. "Yeah, I'm the new Pentagon liaison. Is Dr. Zarkov around?"

A great bear of a man with a close-trimmed beard and a shaved head swam over the lip of the dock module and came halfway through the opening "down" towards us.

"Hello. You are Jenkins? I am Zarkov. I look forward to work with you." His head and shoulders retreated back out of the institutional pale-green capsule, nodding with a massive dignity befitting his legend.

Zarkov was the engineering genius who had <u>finally</u> gotten fusion out of the time-loop it had been stuck in, forever thirty years in the future, and made it a practical technology in the present. His multi-stage approach, like a four-cylinder internal combustion engine of gigantic proportion, used a laser/inertial containment system for the fusing of the first pellet of deuterium, the laser acting as the spark plug. The genius was in the re-cycling of waste heat energy by the encircling shroud of nano-thickness superconductor, and the channeling of that energy back to initiate a cascade of three more tokomak chambers, which in turn charged the colossal laser to re-run the first stage, returning a net gain of energy with every cycle.

Karen Dale's demonstration of genius, six years before, had been to identify in her PhD thesis that the leftover energy from the laser could act as a propulsion vector, and that the shroud could just as well be a sail. Karen moved fast, winning the Nobel in Physics at twenty-four when her collaboration with Zarkov produced a prototype that went to Mars orbit and back in six weeks.

There were dark mutterings by other physicists, not to mention the American government, at her direct sponsorship by Czar Putin, punctuated by regular personal interviews at his private Dacha. But jealousy is the natural reaction of normal people to superior genius. No doubt the Neanderthal wandering the Alpine meadows and forests in the sweet-scented mountain breezes of pre-history nurtured a powerful resentment of those smooth-skinned pipsqueaks who made such fancy spear-throwers out of antler and sinew. With the unlimited material backing of the Russian monarch, her LRPP spaceship drive had toured the Roman pantheon in a triumphal series of tests, crossing the oceanic orbit of Neptune and returning last year.

"Let me show you around, before I take you to your quarters," she said. I followed her through the branching hamster maze of abandoned fuel tanks that is the ISS. Artfully positioned prismatic LED lights gave an energizing vibe to many of the spaces, despite the stark smooth finish of all the surfaces so essential for proper ventilation.

She showed me my work-station, and I stowed my encrypted computing and communications gear. She showed me how to operate negative-pressure trash chutes, how to clip into the wall in case of a depressurization alarm, and gave me the video some wag had entitled "Shitting in Space."

We went to the local watering holes, competing auto-mats with seating consisting only of racks to clip into. One with a spectacular window view of Earth was named Planet Mongo; the other, called Arboria, overlooked the delightful flowering terraced racks of the hydroponics garden. It was 22:00 hours local time, so many of the ISS-natives (or "iss-ants") were dialing up and sucking down chilled pouches of blended tang and liquor.

"All the alcohol is locally distilled," she explained. "We call it Recycled Vodka."

We shared a tasty mango-flavored sorbet, and then she "stood up", unclipping from the rack and tensing to push off once I was ready. "Let me show you the gym, Gordon," she said.

We floated down another corridor into a module that smelled more strongly than the rest of the station of body odor. Karen pulled something in a zip-lock bag from one of the cargo-pouches on her suit, and after unsealing the bag produced with a flourish a bunch of dried lavender.

"I grew this myself, in the public garden section of the hydroponics lab," she said as she deftly secured the stems to a rail along the wall with a twist-tie. "Doesn't it just smell like heaven?"

I found myself jolted back, way back, to a childhood dream of a garden path, a fountain, and a girl so beautiful and cool that it hurt to look at her, who smiled at me in the starlight amid peony and lavender... and then I woke up to find my Dad spraying air-freshener in the hallway.

"Are you all right?" asked Karen, looking over her shoulder from where she had busied herself flicking on the exercise machines.

"Yeah, I'm sorry, it was a long flight, and I'm pretty tired."

"I often find that when I feel tired, what I really need is exercise," she said. "Let me show you how these work."

She proceeded to demonstrate the various exercise machines in zero gravity. "This multi-machine works all the flexors and extensors in your legs," she said, showing me how to attach the straps, where to put my feet, and how to drink from a squeeze bottle, very carefully so as not to spill.

At first I didn't understand her, because I was hypnotized, caught up in the novel sensation of floating, the rhythmic beeping of the machines, the scent of lavender, the smooth movements of her long, lean body, and the memories of childhood dreams. Most of all, I was fascinated by the tiny jewels of sweat catching multi-colored light, weightlessly compounding into a treasury on her skin.

"Uh, beg pardon, Ms. Dale?"

"Call me Karen. I said, do you want me, Gordon?" She had the eyes of a thief: shrewd, active, a little cold. "I've looked you up, mister intelligence agent. You aren't married. You don't even have a girlfriend, do you?"

I suffered a break with reality. I remember sealing the entrance to the gym capsule behind us, and leaping at her, soaring talons outstretched like a springing panther or an eagle in flight. She could have dodged, but instead just watched me with her inscrutable eyes.

Then I became a bank robber breaking into her vault, tearing off her remaining clothes to harvest those jewels of sweat with my tongue.

All the time I was licking, grasping, and gnawing at her like an animal, she was calmly reaching around my back to push us off the ceiling and back towards the rack to clip us in. I will always remember entering her, and the sounds she made, and the furnace-like heat of her body. She got a little mad at me in the end.

"No, God damn it, no, Gordon-- don't pull out. Do you have any idea how long it takes to get semen out of your hair when you can't shower properly? In null-gravity it goes everywhere."

I need to clarify: my job in space was to spy, on the Chinese. After CalTech, there was language school in Arlington, general tradecraft at Camp Perry, finishing school at the American embassy in Beijing. I was an astronomer, a cyber-terrorist, a cryptologist, and a sexually repressed bastard. My trainers were idiots. Karen cracked me in half an hour; all she had to do was tell me what she wanted.

"It's still too slow, Gordon," she explained. We were clipped into the rack at Arboria, looking over the artificial landscape of herbs and flowers, and the tapas menu printed in Cyrillic. "Does the pureed lamb sound good to you?"

"What's too slow?"

"My baby, the Photon, the most wonderful invention in the history of womankind."

"What do you mean, too slow? It's been on the grand tour, to every planet in the solar system. It's a miracle, it's amazing. You're amazing."

"No," she said, now stern. "It's still too slow to reach Centauri. I want to get to the stars."

"Can Zarkov tweak his design?"

She peeled open another vodka and Tang, squeezing it dry into her mouth. "You mean my design. And the answer is no. We just don't accelerate fast enough."

"Well, I'm sorry, but there's nothing I can do to help, Karen."

She shook her head, and her eyes were bright with recycled vodka and a Promethean lust for stolen fire. "You're wrong, Gordon. I need you to get me a meeting with Ming Feng."

Feng was the technocrat in charge of New Beijing, the lunar colony, and the man I'd dedicated three years of my life to profiling. "What does Ming Feng have to do with reaching the stars?" I asked. Then I saw it. The titanic microwave assembly the Chinese used for transmitting solar power down from the moon. She wanted to wind-surf on that. I looked at her face, so brilliant, fierce, and cold. I couldn't refuse her.

I went back to work full time, back to my twenty-hour-a-day schedule, figuring out how to make it happen. Feng's was the face I saw when I looked in the mirror. The profiling training goes so deep, you stop knowing where the subject ends and you begin. Karen pumped me dry.

"What's his favorite animal?" she gasped into my ear.

"Hippo." I grunted. "That's the noise they make when they mate."

She laughed as we bounced around the floor, ceiling, and walls of her sleeping cabin, a sound I'll never hear again but will never forget: like a dirty angel, or a goddess of love.

"What does he want? What does he need? Where is the intersection?" Karen demanded of me, weeks later, fully dressed and impatiently pushing my groping fingers away.

By this time, I was her abject slave. I'd stopped even opening mail from my superiors. My job was to do what Karen wanted.

"He wants the design for <u>Photon</u>. He emotionally needs to dominate. To become emperor," I said, my drug-sharpened, lust-inspired focus hacking new interconnections between my analytical consciousness and the Jungian deep.

"The intersection is--" I winced; a stinging reservoir of sweat had collected against the underside of my upper eye-socket, an annoyance possible only in heaven. "Got it. It's you, Chang'e, the woman in the moon. He'll feel he's living out mythology. He'll give you anything, for making him feel like a god."

"I know he will," she said, glee in her lupine eyes. "Who are you?" she asked.

Rolling with the intensity of the classified, government-synthesized drugs we called "the profiler's little helper," I heard myself answer questions I had no comprehension of. "I'm the jade rabbit."

She nodded to herself, reached into my pants and took me out, then glanced at me with frustration and disgust. "Jesus, Gordon, what have I told you about cumming in zero gravity?"

I worked my contacts, burned three moles, and stopped sleeping all together, tripping on "helper" to get through. I managed to set up a meeting at the L5 point, in a derelict old Mir knockoff the Japanese had built before they fell under the shadow of the Dragon.

Zarkov, Karen, and I arrived first. I had weapons, but didn't think I'd need them. We'd expected a guard for the Chinese contingent, but when the capsule docked and the airlock cycled, only one man stepped through. I stared at on the lone figure stepping into the station, whose features were Gordon Jenkins', and wondered if I'd cracked up for good. Then Ming Feng raised his reflective faceplate.

As Karen and the technocrat sequestered themselves for negotiations, I rested on the bare metal and watched the blowing dust in newly-reactivated HVAC breeze. Zarkov stood like the carved monolith of some long-forgotten empire, eyes unblinking yet unseeing. Over the rattle of the ventilation system I thought I heard moaning.

"Dr. Zarkov, were you ever with Karen?"

The stone figure came to life for a moment. He grunted. "What, you think the chief engineer of Russian spaceflight gives free looks at his blueprints to everyone?"

I watched a tiny dust-devil spawn, twirl, and die. "Why do you stay with her now?" I said.

He regarded me with that special tenderness we offer only to small children and the mad. "Why do you?"

Two weeks later, I received communiqués that sounded panicked even in code, referencing swarms of new Chinese activity on the lunar microwave array. "ARE ... THEY ... BUILDING ... WEAPON?"

"NO," I replied, and destroyed the connection.

Meanwhile, Zarkov and his team went into overdrive, refitting the Photon with an upgraded sail.

Six weeks after that, I was wandering the LRPP complex in the wee hours, mindlessly checking every airlock for safety malfunction. Open, shut; double-check: open, shut, repeat. Helper does weird things to the brain. Behind one maintenance bay door to the Photon, I found a hundred pounds of human jerky: Zarkov dead, without his dignity or a pressure suit, freeze-dried by hard vacuum. His suicide note, scratched into the metal of the airlock in his neat block handwriting so precisely that it might have been etched there by the manufacturer, consisted of only two words in Russian that my language training allowed me to translate as "She's leaving."

"Karen, where are you going?"

Totally unruffled by my surprise entrance into her locked private office, her eyes rolled over me without stopping, still fixed on the farthest shore. "To the stars, Gordon, like I told you."

"I thought you just meant the ship. You mean to pilot it yourself?"

"Of course; who knows it better? You've got to think through the implications of star-flight, Gordon. It means giving humanity a second chance. This is the most important thing anyone has ever done, and I'm going to be the one to do it."

A tsunami of anger washed thought-driftwood onto the beachhead of my mind, and I made another flash connection. I noticed for the first time, I recognized the look of larceny in her eyes from my own. One by one the better angels of my nature fought against my new idea, but fell vanquished into the pit.

"Don't quit your day job," I said. I turned on my heel, overrode her door and communications switches, incapacitated three sentries with low-frequency sonic grenades, buckled and plugged myself into the Photon's controls and life-support systems, and triggered the signal for the Chinese to hit the masers. When the Photon's new sail billowed with harvested sunlight amplified and re-emitted as microwaves, a fat old wooly mammoth named Ten Gees sat on me and crushed the void beneath my sternum.

I thought I might die; but change is good. I blacked out in the navigation couch and slept for seventy-two hours. I was catheterized, and modern med-bots are wonderful. They pumped me full of anti-psychotics and antigens to helper, and I came nearly all the way back; to being no crazier than your average veteran of the Battle of the North China Sea.

When I woke up, I took a sober, sane look at my circumstances, double-checked the course calculations for Proxima Centauri and my life-system supplies, and hit the starter for the brainchild of Hans Zarkov and Karen Dale.

It was a long trip out. Point-three c is fast, but time-dilation doesn't really start until you hit point-nine. Twelve years, more or less. I read a lot. Nothing deep; simplistic, unreflective adventure stories were best. I tried writing, but I lost my feel for people from lack of contact. Math, however, was soothing. I found that working on geometric proofs was just about right for making it through the long stretch.

When I hit the Centauri system, I took a little space-walk, and considered just letting go and floating away, for some alien or God to find me nine billion years or names from now. But then I looked at the stars, from an angle no one else has ever seen. I thought about my parents, and decided that though they did a bad job, I came out alright.

I went back inside, put on "Piper at the Gates of Dawn", and flipped the ship to set up a tight pass around Proxima Centauri, so I could shoot back the way I'd come, harnessing the foreign sun's gravity and solar wind to maximize efficiency for the trip home.

Then just an hour ago, while zipping around another star, first human being ever to do so, thank you very much, I hit a cosmic pothole, my sails tore and my mirror broke. An infinity of bad luck descended. Since then, I've been staring out the window, watching the winking reflections of myself slowly drift away.

The radio, which has spent the whole journey making humpback-whale-song-noises, speaks with Karen's voice.

"Gordon, are you there?"

The leviathan belly-flops on my chest, and it feels like it'll never get off. So I pick up the mike.

"Karen. Yes, I'm here. I suppose you'll get this in four years." Cosmic background static is my lonely, inevitable answer, so I just keep talking. "Why'd you do it all? What made you want the stars so bad? There's not actually anything here. Just a thin, thin haze of the dust, you know, that we'll all return to soon enough.

Another pool has collected weightless and stinging against my eyes, but this time it's of tears. "I guess I just wish you could have given me longer. I know I'm not like you, the smartest person ever-- and beautiful like a goddess and tough and mean as a titanium rattlesnake. But God, when you were good to me, I was happy.

"You know what, forget it. I'm broken down out here, and there's nothing anyone can do about it. I'm a traitor and a thief; and even if I was able to return the ship and come home, big daddy Putin would do terrible things to me anyway. There's just nothing for me anywhere. Goodbye, Karen."

My reflection on the inside of the windshield goes all blurry, the image broken by differential refractions from my tears. I put my head down in silence, ready for the end.

Thirty seconds go by.

"Rattlesnake my ass, Gordon!"

I pick my head back up.

"That's right, I'm less than a light-minute away, you naughty boy. Steal my *Photon*, will you? You think I'd let you be the only one on the statue for the first interstellar humans? I'm calling from the *Forbidden City*; Ming Feng built it from my plans, but I stole his ship too.

"Hang in there; I'll need a day or so to match trajectories with you. We'll dock your command capsule and reactors, and tow you. You've just got to get the big things right, Gordon; don't worry about minutia. Do you really think they won't welcome back the very first starship? You're just too sensitive. Don't worry; we'll talk about it on the way home."

I guess we will.

WHO'S GOT THE TIME?

I'm Herb Johnson, and I'm here to tell you, traveling into the future is no problem. Shoot, everyone does it -- just mostly real slow. But with a hot rod, like a Chronomax 3000, in the blink of an eye you can zoom forward a hundred years, a thousand, a billion. What could go wrong? There's no speed limit.

My twelve-year-old nephew took a solo trip last week, to see the moon get eaten by the sun, five billion years from now. He took a picture, posted it on his homepage. The sun is all flushed and swollen, like a diabetic. Pretty neat. Coming back from the future, it's no problem either, right, 'cause you got that beacon, and it ain't moving.

But going backwards: man, history is a haunted house. It's full of cobwebs, squeaky loose boards, things that can sneak up and eat you; and your whole world, too. Take a bite of the wrong sandwich in the wrong deli at the wrong time, and all the sudden there's no more Pittsburgh? My buddy Randy got ten years from the Time Cops on just those charges, but I mean really, who could've expected <u>that</u>?

They dumped him ten years before time travel was invented. Sure, he came back the next day, but he'd gone bald and paunchy, looking twenty years older. He said he had to spend an extra ten years relative time after Eggsonium invented the machine before he could afford a ride on one back to now. I asked him where he'd done his time, and he told me Pittsburgh. I guess he really liked that deli.

Randy was kind of depressing, after he came back. Said we were wasting Time: there was only so much of it and we were burning it up. I said then why was Professor E. the Time man of the year, if it was such a bad invention? He said, "Man of what year?", and then when I told him he knew very well, something about maybe the Doc not being a man at all. He sounded a little crazy, frankly; we don't hang out much anymore.

Now I read all those stories in grade school, about Morlocks and dinosaurs and butterflies and Presidential elections and all that. I'm here to tell you, they're bunk. There's nothing cursed about time travel. I bet those Time Cops shoot Tyrannosaurs all the time, off duty. Like they say, it's my right as an American to go whenever I want, whenever I want.

But sometimes, I wonder. Returning from the past: man, that's no picnic. Sure, you still got the beacon signal from the timeline you departed... but depending on what you did in the past, it's splitting, into a rainbow of choices.

You ever been to a paint store, trying to match up a sample from your house? It's like that but 10^{10} worse. Might as well hold your nose, close your eyes, and guess, in the end. I know Professor Eggsonium won't like to hear that, but that's what I do, and I suspect most other folks too. Doing it by the book, waiting till you get an exact match: that's so hard, might as well be impossible. And who's got the time?

CONSTRUCTING GUANTANAMO

"So, we're in the middle of doing it, I start playing with her butt-hole, and she just goes crazy! From then on, all she wanted was to be fucked in the ass," Roger shouted, with his mask pulled off his big mouth against regulations so we could all hear his bragging over the thumping of the compressor and the roar of the fans.

"Roger, you are so full of shit," I said, pulling off my own uncomfortable mask for a minute. The dust from the cut drywall clung to our sweat-drenched clothing like a coat of feathers.

Roger lifted his shirt. "Am I, Sam?" His muscular abdomen was covered in small round bruises. "Hickeys, man! Annette's a damn Hoover vacuum. You should see my dick!"

Maybe he wasn't making it up, in which case he was stupider than I thought. He was talking about Lieutenant Cord's wife.

At six the whistle blew. "Miller time!" hollered Dave, my roommate in the converted shipping container with holes for utility access and air conditioners where we slept. Though the idiot loved his neon Miller Lite sign so much I had to threaten him to get him to turn off so I could.

"One week till Jamaica, and <u>weed</u>," Dave said as we walked away from the tool lockers just outside the construction site where we were installing the drop-ceiling. Our employers must have figured we'd explode from boredom if they didn't give us civilian contractors off-base privileges on occasion, so they arranged one flight from Cuba every six weeks.

I laughed. "I'll be on the plane. Just don't try bringing any back. Don't. The month before we got here some guy smuggled some joints back in his shampoo bottle, and after he got caught, the MPs conducted a rectal exam. Then he got fired, sent home to jail, and never even got his last paycheck. Thank you, President Reagan!"

Roger butted in. "Forget about weed; Jamaica's got what you really need. Pussy, Shepherd! Or are you a faggot?" he said.

"Thinking it's stupid to risk jail for tail doesn't make me anything but smart, Roger," I said, and turned away.

"What's that supposed to mean?" I heard him, but I didn't look back. Didn't he realize this wasn't a free country? We weren't in America, we were in Guantanamo. Not that sleeping with other people's wives is OK back home. But here; who knows what they could do to you?

I stripped off my filthy shirt and walked bare-chested downhill through rows of palm trees with wavering fronds the half mile to the beach. Guantanamo Bay has some pretty nice beach. It'd be a lot nicer if it wasn't in the middle of an armed camp with no women you were allowed to touch closer than Key West across 90 miles of the Gulf of Mexico.

Reaching the sand, I further stripped down to my boxers and just fell forward into the gentle surf. Seabirds wheeled overhead, riding the evening breeze. This was indeed paradise… for a man without balls.

"Hey, Sammy," said a voice of gravel and stone. "Get out for a minute; I need to talk to you."

I looked up, and saw Uncle Vin.

Uncle Vin got me this job last Christmas, when I was camped out on my Mom's couch having run out of money for college after one semester. Dad was supposed to hook me up for the spring term, but he didn't. Dad never really came all the way back from Vietnam. Last I heard, he'd lost his job at the steel mill in Baltimore and was back on the sauce.

My mom bitched at me every day.

"You're not a little kid anymore, Sam. I got to look out for myself, now. I leave for work and you're here sitting on your ass, I come home and you're still there, and all the milk and Steakums are gone. Get a job, or join the Hari Krishnas, but Jesus do something, because you are not staying forever on my couch!"

One day, I woke up to find her looming over me at six in the morning.

"Go away Mom, I'm still asleep."

"Get up, Sam," she said.

"Mom, it's still night-time. I'll go down to the job center later today."

"You'll get up now, you lazy brat," she said, and the crazy bitch poured a whole pitcher of orange juice on my head.

That night, Uncle Vin came over.

"Let's go have a beer, Sammy, what do you say?"

Was this my eviction notice? I glanced at Mom, who'd stopped acting crazy but who also hadn't apologized. She nodded. "Go on, Sam, it's alright, don't worry about waking me up when you get home, I'm going to be at Frank's tonight. I'll talk to you tomorrow, OK?"

Her purple-lined eyes looked sad, and old. I felt too disgusted to stay furious at her.

"Ok, Mom, Ok, Uncle Vin. Let me get my coat. Where are we going?"

"What do you care? I'm buying."

That was Uncle Vin in a nutshell. We went to Joseph's, his favorite bar and virtual office. Dank and smoky, they sold quarter drafts four till seven weekdays. We sat facing each other in the booth, and after drinking fifty cents worth each in silence, the pressure got to me.

"So, what's up, Uncle Vin? Did Mom call you and tell you to get rid of me?"

My voice quavered and broke. Vincent Giambi was an enormous man, thick and tall, taking more after the Croatian blood in the family than the Italian. He was ten years older than Mom, her half-brother. He was in construction, had grown up in Italy in the forties and fifties, apprenticed to stonemasons since early childhood, rebuilding the ruins. The family rumor was he'd had to leave the old country after killing communist agitators as a strike-breaker, but made connections here in Philly and brought Grandma and Mom over within two years.

He stared at me for another agonizing moment, bushy black eyebrows drawn together over his massive nose, and shook his head.

"No. Your Mom, she's a good lady. She loves you, dumb-ass. When she called me today, she said, 'Vincent, please get Sammy a job, he's a smart boy, he can help your business.' So, I've been sitting here looking at you, trying to see your smarts. Nothing so far."

I felt a sting, but I ignored it.

"What kind of job, Uncle Vin, construction?"

He snorted. "Yeah, construction. What do you think I do? What other business do I have?"

I wasn't touching that one. "None I ever heard of, Uncle Vin. What I meant was, yes, I would love to work for your construction business. When can I start?"

He flashed a sign to the bartender, who brought us a couple shots. Uncle Vin smiled, for the first time I could remember. "Now, there's the Sam Shepherd smarts I heard so much about. You get your stuff together tonight, and meet me at my office tomorrow morning at six o'clock. Don't be late. Here's ten bucks for the cab. You pack all you'll need for nine months, but make sure it all fits in one bag, and bring that bag with you. No more than twenty pounds."

"How do I know what twenty pounds is, Uncle Vin; and, why?"

He raised his glass to me, and said "Your mom's got a scale in her bathroom, kid."

Oh, yeah. I clinked and gulped with him. As I blinked and shook my head, he answered my other question.

"Because, Sam, you're going to Cuba."

As he explained to me at his office the next morning, Vincent Giambi Construction Inc. was a subcontractor to the Bechtel corporation for the project of expanding the infrastructure on the US military base at Guantanamo Bay, Cuba.

This was the deal: general construction work six till six, six days a week, with twenty minutes off the clock for lunch. It was seventy hours a week, fifteen dollars an hour, tax free, plus room and board. A fucking fortune; with this I could make enough money for the rest of college and then some, in less than a year. I actually cried when Uncle Vin told me. He hugged me, but gave me a warning, with a hand on my shoulder, and a salami-sized finger waggling in my face.

"Do not screw this up, Sammy. This is business, now. Not just family. Be smart enough not to get in trouble down there, or I will kick your ass," he said. I nodded.

"Sam, I get these contracts because of reputation. My workers don't make trouble, see? That's how the Navy likes it. I hire young guys like you because you can work hard twelve hours a day and not break down. But the problem is, the Navy doesn't pay as good as this."

"No shit," I said, having researched that option early on in my stint on mom's couch.

"I mean, not even the officers. Not by half. The only reason we pay this much is, my company gets paid at twice our costs. Do you understand? The more I pay my workers, the higher figure I can multiply when I present them with my bill."

The insight floored me: you don't get paid for the intrinsic worth of what you do. You get paid as a side effect, depending on how much what you are doing does for someone else. It's one of the best lessons anyone's ever given me, but it was only the second most important thing I learned the year I worked construction at Guantanamo.

"So, you get three times the money for hanging drywall twelve hours a day that these guys make for risking their lives 24/7. It leads to bad feelings. Understand that.

This is a small town you are moving to for nine months, surrounded by barbed wire and Cubans with guns. There is nowhere to hide, no room to avoid people."

"So?"

"Listen, dumbass. The officers bring their wives and families to live here. So the only women there are some officer's wife; the only girls there are some officer's daughter. If you touch any pussy there, it will cause trouble. If the Navy heard that Giambi Construction workers cause trouble, they would tell Bechtel to stop hiring me. That would make me upset. Do not do such a thing, Sam. Do you understand? Watch the other ones, too."

I waded back out of the surf towards my uncle's long silhouette against the purple and gold sunset. "Uncle Vin! What are you doing here?"

He handed me a towel. "I'm just here for some meetings. Pick up your stuff and let's take a walk. Tell me about the worksite. Are you guys on schedule? Is the work good? Are people staying out of trouble?"

"Oh, yeah, everything's fine," I said. I don't know why I would cover for Roger, it just happened. I guess saying nothing seemed easier.

He looked me up and down. "OK. Make sure you call me if things go off the rails. I am counting on you to be my eyes and ears, remember that. You look good, Sam. You've filled out from the work. You been saving your money?"

"What could I possibly spend it on?"

He nodded. "That's a good boy. So, how about the tools? I got them from a new supplier this time, and…"

Our conversation progressed though various boring topics, and I submerged my unease at lying. I was as clean as the driven snow. Roger, he was his own problem.

The next morning, Annette Cord came to the work site, trailed by her daughters Hannah and Heather, ages six and four.

"Hi Roger," she said in the dead silence that followed her arrival. She was unbelievable. Like Christy Brinkley. She was Swedish, almost six feet tall, and sexy: blond, slim, with huge boobs and an unforgettable ass - one which, thanks to Roger, I couldn't help thinking of what it would be like to fuck.

Her ass was on public display in the shortest of all possible denim shorts. Her boobs were held back only by a scarlet tube top. Dave Peterson broke the silence by craning his neck so far to look while still walking in his stilts as to clock himself on a hanging pipe. Our laughter broke the spell, and we pretended to go back to work.

While she traded innuendo with Roger, I couldn't take my eyes off the little kids. They looked like angels, with golden curls and the most innocent faces imaginable. They were dressed in matching little pretend tennis outfits. They stood right there watching their beautiful flirt with a stupid, greasy roughneck who was not their dad.

I walked forward, and took a yo-yo out of one of my many pockets. Yes, I know it's juvenile, but I sometimes I just like doing something with my hands.

"Hi, girls," I said. "Would you like to see a trick?"

They looked at one another solemnly, and then both nodded. "Yes, please," said the older one.

So I showed them walk the dog, and round the world, and then I stopped, because their mom had come over to watch me play with her kids.

"Hi, my name's Sam," I said. "Nice kids."

She looked at me, one eyebrow raised. "Don't mess with my kids, yo-yo man, or my husband will blow your brains out."

"You got it all wrong, lady. I was just..." What had I been doing, anyway?

"Playing, I see that. I was just testing you." She smiled, and I flushed. "See you later, Sam," she said, and walked off with her two girls trailing behind like ducklings.

She came by one other time during the week, and I again felt compelled to distract her kids, as if yo-yo tricks could somehow insulate them against the treacheries of the adult world. Was my nice-guy act just a ploy to get a beautiful woman's attention? I admit it's a possibility.

That Friday, Dave and I were standing on the tarmac waiting for our flight to Kingston.

"Where's Roger?" I said. "What the hell is keeping him?"

"He ain't coming," said Dave. "He said he wasn't feeling good, wanted to rest up for next week."

Maybe he just couldn't think of anything in Jamaica that was better than what he was getting right here in Guantanamo. But he was taking a hell of a risk. Lt. John Cord, USMC, was not someone I would want to tangle with.

I saw a figure approaching the airstrip out of the dusk. It was Uncle Vin. He motioned me over, out of the other guys' earshot.

"I just wanted to see you before I went back tomorrow. Things are good, Sam. I got a contract extension for another eighteen months."

"All right, that's great."

"You done good here, kid. When you get back, come see me before you go off to school."

"Sure thing. I'll see you in September."

He nodded, and walked away. Then the plane readied for takeoff, and we went to Jamaica.

Jamaica was fun, but nothing you need to hear about; besides, a lot of it is pretty fuzzy anyway- all clouded by smoke, as it were. Anyways, we came back, and worked our shifts, and Annette kept coming by, sometimes the worksite during the day with her kids to flirt, sometimes to our trailer park at night to screw Roger, judging by the sounds of it. Shipping containers don't have a whole lot of sound-proofing. Time went by.

Roger didn't go to Jamaica the next month, either. Nor the next. As August rolled around, I began to think that Annette's husband must be blind, deaf, or dead. How could he not know?

One early morning, I got shaken awake in the dark.

"Nephew, put on a shirt and shoes and come with me, now." His whisper was calm and quiet, but I was terrified. I threw on a Baja and loafers by the light of the Miller sign and followed Uncle Vin out into the tropical night, leaving Dave still snoring in the upper bunk. A few paces away from the trailer, he whirled and confronted me.

"I thought you were going to keep an eye out for me. Didn't we agree on that, when I hired you?"

"What do you mean — aarggh!" His slap left my face numb.

"I mean I want you to take these keys, go to your about-to-be-fired friend's trailer, collect the lieutenant's wife, and drive her home. Then, you pack your stuff. Maybe your worthless father never taught you, but when you make a deal, you need to hold up your own end. Didn't I tell you that reputation matters? Didn't you think that when I said 'no pussy' I meant everybody, not just you?" He shook his head in disgust.

"What's happened here is, money breaks people down. People with weak characters, they forget what's important, they put all their dreams into money, like if they had more, they'd be happy. Like you, you cried because I gave you this job. Weak."

"Will you tell me what happened, Uncle Vin? Why are you so upset?"

He grabbed my shirt-front and shook me till my teeth clacked. "Because that woman has two little girls, and her husband made her a whore, and it makes me sick. So, go take her home. Right now." He dropped my shirt and I ran for Roger's trailer.

When I got to there, Roger was nowhere to be seen, but Annette stood by the lamppost out front, in shorts and a windbreaker.

"I guess you're my ride," she said.

"Where's Roger?"

"The MP's just took him away."

"What for?"

She looked at me sidelong.

"I mean, that isn't a crime, really, is it?"

She let out a sigh. "I don't know, you Americans are all crazy about sex. I think I got Roger in bad trouble. I guess I'm a bitch."

I thought I saw tears, but I couldn't be sure in the dim lamp-light.

I pointed to the jeep Uncle Vin had parked there. "Shall we go?"

"OK, yo-yo man."

After we started moving through the pre-dawn streets of a little pretend town, she turned towards me in the front seat. "So, I think I maybe am in bad trouble now, also. John, too."

"What about your kids, lady?" It just burst out of me.

She nodded. "Sam, right? That is your name? I will tell you what. Heather and Hannah, I love them. They will be part of me forever. I want nothing but good for them. But what about me? How can I live, here? When I met John it was very exciting. He is handsome, foreign; I show him around Europe, there are clubs and cafes, and culture. We make love a lot, and life is an adventure.

"But now, John never touches me. We live in a prison, and there is no adventure. And the girls, they are prison, too, yes? There is no culture, there is just – nothing. I did not want this life. I don't love Roger, he is stupid. I just want to feel something, anything. I am dead, here; I need to leave. Leave Roger, leave John, leave Cuba. Goodbye, I am done."

We pulled up at her house, and I was drowning in memories. My Mom, young and glamorous, and me, trailing snottily behind, left at home when she went out late and came home early. The dozens of boyfriends, the shitty apartments… and my Dad.

Lt. Cord sat in the moonlight on the front stoop of his neat bungalow, inside the square white picket fence around his yard, smoking a cigar with a half-empty bottle of whisky in his hand.

"You're home late, honey," he said to Annette.

She turned to me, eyes wide. "Leave, please, Sam."

I don't know why, but I shut off the car, got out of the driver seat, and approached the gate.

"Sir, I just want you to know that –"

"Who the hell are you?"

"Sam Shepherd." I waited a couple of beats, then added "A construction worker. My uncle -"

He cut me off again. "Another fix-it man, Annette? What is it about those handy men, huh?" He was off the steps and brushing past me before I realized it.

"John, let go of me. I will get out, just let me go."

I bounced up, adrenaline pumping. Nine months of construction had made me strong. I reached for his back. "Lieutenant Cord - aeuggh." He gave me a perfect donkey kick to the gut. I sat back on the sidewalk and concentrated on trying to breathe.

She was out of the car now, white-faced in the glare of the street-lamps. He had her by both shoulders as he marched her backwards through the gate and towards the house.

"Before I go, you are going to tell them. Tell the girls why mommy and daddy won't be living together any more."

I was a helpless witness, sucking wind.

"Ok, John, I'll say it: because Daddy took money from a man to let him keep sleeping with Mommy-"

He struck her then, and she fell whimpering onto the sidewalk. I finally caught my breath and staggered towards him, hands raised palms outwards.

"Hey, hey, don't do it, man. Think of those kids!" I said, knowing from experience that little faces were peeking out of the window, helpless to keep from seeing the end of their family, to them the end of the world.

He stared at me. "She was fucking a mechanic, man," he said.

"A dumb redneck who makes four times what I do, for hanging drywall. So, I told him: 'Fine, you can have her, and keep your job... as long as I get half your paycheck.' Just to even things out."

It finally dawned on me what they'd been saying, and why Roger had been skipping the Jamaica runs: he couldn't afford them anymore. "You mean, you pimped out your wife?"

I turned a fraction, to make eye contact with Annette. Then a hand spun my shoulder back around, and he hit me hard, between my right cheekbone and nose. I felt something crack.

I looked up from the ground, covered in blood, but the attack was suspended as Cord finished his bottle of Cutty Sark. "My career is over. My God," he said. With a vicious throw he shattered the empty bottle against the front steps in a geyser of glass. From inside the house, the sound of terrified children became audible.

"Forget your career, Cord," I said. "Try thinking about your kids, you asshole." I got to my feet, and grabbed his arms. I heard Annette run by me up the stairs and the door slam. As we wrestled, it crossed my mind that he would kill me before she summoned the MPs. I didn't care.

He broke my grip and threw me over his shoulder. I waited for the kick, but it didn't come. I looked up, and saw Cord enveloped by a massive shadow pinning both his arms in a full nelson.

"You want I should break both arms, or only the one?" grated Uncle Vin. Then Cord howled as a strike-breaker re-lived the good old days. I laughed for a second; then I started to cry. My face was killing me, and my mind was flashing back. Back to my father in the same pose, when Vincent removed him from Thanksgiving when I was thirteen. I wondered at the tapestry of fate, that some patterns repeat so exactly. I heard sirens, and Annette and the girls in fear, and now John Cord in pain, and I put my face in the grass and sobbed.

Uncle Vin said later he was sorry he put me in that spot; that's another first, him apologizing. I told him I was sorry he lost the contract with the Navy. Bechtel did chuck Giambi Construction over the side; I heard that the military wives pay-for-play scandal almost made Sixty Minutes until somebody hushed it up. He shrugged, and said it was just business- but that he would never hire me again.

He didn't say why he made me take Annette home, or why he followed me out to the house. Maybe it was his way of getting me the ass-kicking he promised me if I fucked up. But at least he made sure I wasn't killed, which I appreciate.

I'm glad as hell that I got that job at Guantanamo. The money changed my life, and I learned a few things too, both about money and not. It's funny how Roger got the booty and I got the beat-down; what's not funny is that I still think about Annette, all the time. I wonder what happened to her, and those two cherubs trailing behind her. At least I taught those little girls how to yo-yo, and made them smile. Sometimes, that's all you get a chance to do. I guess I can live with that.

I called Mom when I got back to Philly. Classes started in two days, and I had a crooked nose and spectacular shiner. But I was pretty happy. I told her I was going to make the Dean's list this semester, and I meant it. It just felt good talking to her, for the first time in forever. I'd have called Dad too, if I had a number for him. Maybe he'll show up for my graduation.

WHY DOES SHE NOT JUST RIP OFF HIS HEAD, AND THEN FEED?

When Captain John Smith came and told me he was leaving forever, after loving me one last time, I ran weeping to tell my father that I had for two years given my body and soul to the Englishman's keeping.

My father laughed bitterly, and gestured from his high chair down the length of his warm lodge. Regular smoke-holes pierced the gloom with shafts of sunlight, revealing dozens of warriors and wise men attendant on Wahunsunacawh, the Emperor Powhatan of Tenakomakah.

"Does my daughter think Chief Powhatan needs even one of his medicine men to discern the heart of a girl? No, Pocahontas, there will be no revenge for your honor against Smith and the English today. For your honor was no more than part of my tribute to them."

My father grabbed me by the hair as I turned to run away, perhaps to drown myself as I felt drowned already by despair and shame. "Listen to me, daughter of my heart. These are hard truths, but a warrior must be strong, must endure the wrongs of his enemy until he is ready and able to strike back well. A snake that strikes too soon starves to death. Can you be a girl like the warrior: not let your hurt starve you, but feed you?"

I wiped my eyes, and gave a little nod.

"Good. You <u>must</u> be so; I have a plan which needs you. This is Tomocomo who speaks to the fish, the bird, the beaver, and to man: he is a shaman from a tribe far, far away, and his medicine is very strong."

A stranger stood forth from the gloom in the back of the lodge, far from any of the beams of sunlight. "Hello Pocahontas, I am Tomocomo, Speaker-To-Animals," he said. "Would you like to be my pupil?" Before the stern and eager face of my father, I nodded, and the deal was struck.

He spoke the Algonquian language of our people, but he was not of our tribe, nor any I had seen before or since. He often seemed only the semblance of a man, like a shaman might wear the mask and fur of a bear or mastodon to share its essence. As he crossed the hall he could not help but cross at least one sunbeam, and when he did I am certain that the shadow cast upon the floor was in no way human.

"Tomocomo will awaken the totem spirit in you, to give you the strength to fight and right the English wrongs, and drive them from our land," said my father.

After running his hands over my face and limbs, Tomocomo pronounced my doom. "She looks like… a wolf, I think," said the stranger who looked like nothing at all. Such was my beginning on the journey into skin-changing.

He took me, and taught me, and scarred, blooded, and shaped me, until by the light of the full moon I was not Pocahontas the maiden but a monster. A wolf, but of great size, and not quite the same as those I knew.

Meanwhile, to further ripen his plan, my father arranged for my marriage to another English John, this one Rolfe. He was kind but weak, and his caresses in the dark scarce waked me, let alone the passion I had felt with John Smith.

So years passed. I lived with the white men, and they grew more, and we red men less. We were blighted, as the forest was felled; the fish were caught, birds shot, beasts skinned, and our people slaughtered without provocation. My father was forced from cold magic plotting to declare open war against the English, but without hope: in battle their fire-sorcery was too much for his braves' courage. My father made peace at a price, again and again.

When I was twenty, my father called me to him and told me the time had come at last.

"Daughter, Tomocomo and his people can see far past tomorrow or the day after, to the multitude of days that are not come but yet might be, which fall one by one to mulch the ground of the present in the forest of what is possible. His tribe knows seldom-trod paths through that forest of time, and for reasons of their own have shared their lore with me."

"So?" I said.

"We are the enemies of the English now, but Tomocomo says that his tribe shall be their opponent in some of the days that may yet come. At his offering, we have made a pact: you are to strike a blow against our enemy now, at their point of weakness, like smothering the infant heir to an enemy Chiefdom in the cradle. Do you understand?"

I understood that I was an unhappy woman with something to prove to Captain John Smith. So when my father said that Tomocomo would accompany Mr. and Mrs. John Rolfe and some others of the colony back to England, I agreed to the plan without reservation, despite that my part was to be a wolf in London, to terrorize and destroy once and future English enthusiasm for all New Worlds by slaying their king James.

The trip across the sea was terrible. My husband and I as the guests of honor slept in an overgrown cabinet called a cabin. Though the rest of my countrymen who accompanied us as exhibits for the Virginia Colony were able to sleep even on the vomit-soaked floor of the hold, I in my cabin was not. As the moon rising over the water each evening fattened towards full, I wondered how was I, on board ship, to hide my transformations? My experience was that to resist that call of nature, like any other, is painful in the short term, and impossible in the long.

Tomocomo was busy, however. Many nights I heard him over my husband's snores, creep by in the narrow corridor, up the ladder and through the hatch onto the deck. One night, to relieve my tedium and distract my worried mind, I followed him. In the nearly-full moonlight that called out to me like a choir, I caught a glimpse of something man-shaped but fish-white lowering itself over the side. The man at watch stood nearby but snored on his feet.

"Teacher," I said, "where are you bound?"

He smiled, and I saw that his mouth was terrible, a hungry display of saw-edged fangs. "Why, to swim with the fishes, my dear pupil," he said. "This is a side-matter that need not concern you. But you should be glad to know that from tonight forward, the white man's dominion over the ocean will no longer go unchallenged."

Then he released his grip, and something fell into the sea with a mighty splash. I believe that night Tomocomo spawned those great leviathans of the deep that have so harassed European shipping in the years since.

Once landing in Plymouth, we went to various town and country parties, everywhere boosting our dear old Jamestown and Virginia. Tomocomo conducted a census, categorizing every English man or machine he encountered. My husband took me to Norfolk and introduced me to his family at Heacham Hall, who greeted earnest John Rolfe's choice of a wife openmouthed and aghast. My other countrymen in the delegation were even more miserable than on ship, where they had needed only to dodge one-another's spew, not brick-a-brats thrown by the sharp-eyed, strong-armed, English everyman, a great hater of strange skins.

In my own strange skin, I roamed the country under the witnessing moon, devouring any I spied with my own sharp eyes, no matter how strong their arms. Every morning, Tomocomo took a report of my predations, the better to tally his inventory. In fairness, some of the whites were kind enough. But most weren't.

In August, our Virginia embassy was treated to a great entertainment at the Summer Palace in Whitehall, Ben Jonson's masque *The Vision of Delight*. I was entranced, though my husband slumbered from the first act onwards, and Tomocomo kept distracting me with questions reflecting less an unfamiliarity with European customs than with basic human motivations.

"Why does she not merely rip off his head, and then feed?" he asked at one point.

Why not, indeed? Part of me understood his confusion. Then in a flash I saw I had let a false-faced abomination remake me in accordance with its own impulses. I reacted with a sob of self-loathing.

I rose quickly, my world crumbling around me. Leaving Tomocomo to his puzzlement and my husband to his mild, placid dreams, I fled our balcony headless of my direction. In the stairwell I ran headlong into John Smith.

"Why Pocahontas," he exclaimed. "Or rather, Mrs. Rolfe. I was just informed you were here, and was on my way up to see you."

I stammered, blushed, and burst into tears.

"What's the matter?" he asked as we stood there, together on the polished marble stair of a palace, every equal in splendor to the land of wonders that he had always described England to be. I felt myself transported for a moment back into my younger, innocent self.

He was older now, plump and softer than the swift and powerful creature beneath whose overmastering touch I had thrilled as a girl. Now it was I who was swift and powerful, and especially soft and quivering seemed the point just there upon his neck which throbbed in time to the beats of his heart.

Just past my old lover's fragile, pulsing throat I saw the moon. Framed by the grand marble scrollwork around the stairwell window, beaming down through what Tomocomo had taught me was a hundred thousand leagues of airless darkness, my wild bright mistress called to me. It would be but a moment's work to clasp John Smith to myself in a last embrace, and take him with me through the window into the dark encircling palace woods, to enjoy his spurting love one last time... before I ripped off his head and began to feed.

No. No, the horror that gripped me was absolute, and I saw John Smith for what he really was, a man much like my father: a leader, a user, but now old and weakening, and subject at least to some variety of love. And I saw that I still returned that love in some way, as I loved and do love all men so flawed as they are.

But the hunger of the outer dark was very strong in me. I know not what might have happened if Isaac hadn't stepped out and interposed himself between me and John.

"Ah, Captain Smith, is this the fabled Indian princess who once saved your life? Madam, I am Isaac Laquedem, potential financier of your colony of Virginia."

His resurrection of that banal fable was enough to tip the balance of my humors from horror to annoyance. "Pleased to make your acquaintance, Mr. Laquedem. But Mr. Smith invented that story to increase subscription to the Colony. No, I'm just a native girl the Captain wet his Willey in, and gave a good Rodgering like a British tar should. Love them, then leave them; isn't that right, Mr. Smith?"

John looked old then, and sad. "Begging your pardon, Mrs. Rolfe. Might we let bygones be bygone? How is Wahunsunacawh your father? I remember him well. I understand that thanks to your good works, there is peace and trade between the English and the Tenakomakah, as I had always hoped."

"My father is a sick, weak old man, accounted a puppet of the white oppressors by the best of his own people. If he lasts another year as Chief, I shall be surprised."

"For shame! He's a good man, how sad to hear his own daughter speak so ill of him," he said.

"For my part, Mr. Smith, the way I feel about you both is very much the same. Well, good night and good bye, dear old John. Mr. Laquedem, what brings you to this event?" I said, forever turning my back on John Smith and the girlhood he'd dominated.

I was drunk with relief, and felt a buoyancy like that of a diver for shellfish who, after having dropped her bundle of rocks, shoots back up from the oyster reef at the bottom of the bay. Isaac Laquedem took my arm, and we passed into the lavish hall containing the reception line.

"The play is nearly over, my dear. How would you like to meet the King?" he said.

We took a refreshment of Madeira as we queued, and Isaac was charming. I laughed helplessly at his droll character studies of the assembled gentry. When we came to the head of the line, I looked in vain for a regal presence behind the plainly dressed, hatless clerk who greeted us.

"My liege, let me state what a great honor it is as a Jew to have your courtesy directed to me. And might I also congratulate you on your triumphant project to re-arrange and translate the holy writ," said Isaac to the clerk.

"Thank you," the little man said with a smile. "That is indeed to be my greatest work."

"My lord, King James, may I present my escort, the lady Rebecca Rolfe, before marriage the Indian Princess Pocahontas, daughter of the Emperor Powhatan?"

"Ahem," hissed Tomocomo, appearing suddenly at my other elbow from nowhere. "I am the proper escort of the lady. She has perhaps become lost and confused; I hope she has not forgotten her duties?"

With his presence came my hunger rising like a living, corporal thing, and I was re-immersed in the plan. My only desire was to change, to unleash the wildness that lived deep in my breast, to shed my soft meek skin and sink my fangs in the face of the little Englishman until they met deep within his skull. Slaver filled my mouth, and madness my mind. One breath, one more and I should have been lost.

But Isaac patted my hand and spoke. "The lady has forgotten nothing, foreigner; it is you who have forgotten your place." He bowed to the king, helping guide my shaking limbs to essay an acceptable curtsey, and marched me away from where the baleful Tomocomo had stood. But when I looked back I could not see him any longer, though the light of the chandelier was bright.

When we had escaped the reception hall, Isaac walked me back up to the stairwell where he had found me.

"You should find your husband still in your booth there, I think," he said.

"Thank you," I gasped, and kissed his hand. I felt once again the possibility of being clean.

"You are welcome indeed, Mrs. Rolfe," he said. "I must bid you farewell to attend some business, but I will see you again ere you depart London."

"Farewell until then," I said. We waved goodbye as he descended the stairs out of sight, and I turned and straightened my shoulders to resume the burden of wifely duty. But I was never to bear that burden again.

Returning to our balcony, I found my husband alone and still deeply asleep. As I attempted to wake him, Tomocomo spoke from the seat next to me, where he had not been sitting a moment before.

"You meddle in affairs too big for you, little she-wolf," he said, looking at me with his yellow, inhuman eyes. As always a faint trace of scent clung to him; something that since visiting the Rolfe's family crypt, I now recognized as redolent of the mortuary: the smell of frankincense and myrrh.

"It is again as it was so long ago at the juncture of the three continents: inexplicable meddling. This is unacceptable! Do you understand that you have caused me to lose face? I must now make report to my brother in art the Tree of Smoke, and our father the Keeper of the Forest Gate."

"What are you really?" I asked. You are no more Croatan than an Englishman. You're more spider than man."

His eyes then did indeed seem to multiply, as if his invisible masque had slipped. "Foolish girl, I taught you, and shaped you, and skinned you, and made you strong. And this rebellion is how you would repay Tomocomo, Speaker-To-Animals? Bah! Here is my last gift to you, filth: enjoy it well."

Then he took me in his arms, and placed the abyss hidden by his lips against my brow. And then again was I the oyster girl, except this time a bundle of rocks had twined a cord around my ankle as it slipped overboard, and I was sucked down, farther and farther not stopped by the mud at bottom but still falling free through endless squirming muck, until the end of the world.

I lingered in agonizing delirium for weeks, and doctors were brought, but there was never any hope. So died Rebecca Rolfe, Husband of John Rolfe, daughter of Wahunsunacawh. John and the rest of the delegation buried me in the parish of Saint George's in Gravesend, and flew a black flag as the pilot guided them down the widening length of the Thames. They returned over the ocean to Virginia, where my father lived a few months past hearing of my death, bearing the signs of a broken heart.

I woke up to another kiss. It was dark, and I felt cold and wet. I opened my mouth to scream, thinking a man assaulted me in my sleep.

"Shhh," said Isaac, holding up a hooded lantern so I could see his face. "I don't want to wake the cemetery watchman. Can you get up?"

I cautiously stretched out my arms and felt for a purchase on the curious wooden platform I was sleeping on. My fingers touched the walls of a pit to my either side, and I realized: I was in my open coffin, on a dark and rainy night, and I was alive again after death.

Isaac was liberally covered in mud, even his beard and long hair tied back under his skullcap. He was the most handsome man I'd seen in my life.

"This is not Paradise?" I said, fairly sure.

"Oh, no indeed," he said. "The food here is rather bad, for one thing. No, you are still in London."

"How did this happen? How am I alive?"

"I, Isaac Laquedem, wandering Jew born in Bethany, whose mother named him Lazarus, dug you from the peaty churchyard soil and pressed upon you the kiss of life," he said, smiling.

"But… that doesn't make sense. How could you do it, were you even who you say," I asked.

He shrugged. "You know our friend His Majesty is making a new, definitive version of the Book? Well, he left out a few parts."

"Help me up," I said. "I'm really hungry."

"Of course, Rebecca."

"Oh, that's not me. She's dead," I said, with certainty, taking his hand and scrambling up the muddy slope.

"Well then what should I call you?" he said, handing me a spare shovel and gesturing that we should begin to re-cover the grave of Rebecca Rolfe.

I laughed, and stretched in preparation of working beside my handsome Isaac. "My marriage is over, and Rebecca is dead. So is Pocahontas." I smiled, my eyes merry, my teeth long, white, and very

sharp. "You can call me Ms. Wolfe."

THE END

Made in the USA
Middletown, DE
31 October 2021

50824506R00087